DURIN
HER MAJESTY URE

BY

M. E. BRADDON

AUTHOR OF

"LADY AUDLEY'S SECRET," "VIXEN," "LONDON PRIDE," ETC.

COPYRIGHT EDITION

British Library Cataloguing-in-Publication Data
A catalogue record for this book is available from
the British Library

Mary Elizabeth Braddon

Mary Elizabeth Braddon was born in Soho, London, England in 1835. She was educated privately in England and France, and at the age of just nineteen was offered a commission by a local printer to produce a serial novel "combining the humour of Dickens with the plot and construction of G. P. R. Reynolds" What emerged was *Three Times dead, or The Secret of the Heath,* which was published five years later under the title *The Trail of the Serpent* (1861).

For the rest of her life, Braddon was an extremely prolific writer, producing more than eighty novels, while also finding time to write and act in a number of stage plays. Her most famous novel, *Lady Audley's Secret,* began serialisation in 1862, and was an overnight success, propelling her into fame and fortune. A quintessential 'sensation novel', centring on an incident of "accidental bigamy," *Lady Audley's Secret* has never been out of print, and was adapted as recently as 2000. Braddon also founded *Belgravia Magazine,* and edited *Temple Bar Magazine.* She died in 1915 in Richmond, England, aged 79.

DURING HER MAJESTY'S PLEASURE.

THE PROLOGUE.

"I DON'T mind a woman being ever so erratic—as you call it—if she is beautiful, and warm-hearted, and generous," said the doctor.

"No more do I," answered the lawyer, "if she isn't my wife. I admit that Lady Chilworth is handsome—one of the handsomest women I know—and I am quite willing to take your word for her warmth of heart and generosity."

"I knew her in Italy before she was Lady Chilworth," said the doctor.

"Then you know who she was, and why Chilworth married her," said the lawyer eagerly.

"I know that she was a good woman—and worthy

of his affection. If you want to know more than that you must ask Chilworth."

"The Judge did not oblige the witness to reply to the last question," said Henry Halstead, Q.C., laughing. "Upon my soul, Rayson, you are as close about the lady as if she were a case."

"She is a case—for me: the case of an unappreciated wife."

"Rot! The husband showed his appreciation by marrying her—she ought to be satisfied with that, if she was a nobody."

"The kind of nobody all London was talking about last season. Lady Chilworth was the social success of the year, and her husband is the only man I know who isn't in love with her."

"The man has been spoilt by too much luck," said Halstead. "He was a very decent chap when we three men were at Trinity together. Everybody liked him. He was eating his dinners, and cramming law while he worked for the Tripos, as poor as Job, and a glutton for work. That was the only fault anybody found with him. I lost sight of him for years after I left the 'Varsity—heard he had chucked law and taken up literature—heard no more of him till his grandfather died, and left him everything—three or four cousins having dropped off in the interval—for he seemed out of the running when I knew him."

"Yes. There was a consumptive taint in the elder branch of the family, inherited from the mother—an heiress and a beauty, who died in her thirtieth year."

"Well, I envy him his houses and land, but I don't envy him his wife. She is too fiery a spirit for me—wanting to jump over the moon one day—down in the dumps the day after. And I believe she worries him. He has an air of never knowing what she is going to do next."

"Never knowing what she is going to do next," echoed a piping voice, as a slim little man came into the gun-room, out of the rain, slipped out of a long mackintosh, and shook himself in front of the wide hearth, like a dog. A bright-eyed little man, with sleek brown hair and teeth that flashed in the firelight. "You were talking of Lady Chilworth," shaking a finger at Halstead. "Don't deny it. Nobody ever knows what that woman will do next. What do you suppose was her latest performance?"

"She talked of going for a walk after lunch. Not a very eccentric notion," answered Dr. Rayson, dropping the end of his cigar into the ashes and rising from his seat in the ingle nook, with an air of having done with hearth and room now that Reginald Honeybill, everybody's Reggie, had arrived upon the scene. "I conclude that as it has rained cats and dogs all the afternoon, she changed her plans."

"A very reasonable conclusion about any other woman, but not about Lady Chilworth. What do you think of her tramping to the Post Office at Spofforth, four miles from here, alone and in a tempest of rain and wind!"

"I suppose it was no more odd for her to have business at the Post Office, than for you."

"Her husband did not take it so easily. He is not the best tempered man I know, but I never saw him in such a rage as he was in this afternoon. He was driving me home in his cart, after a poor day's sport, and went a mile or two out of his way—a mile and a bittock the Scotch groom called it—to get his letters at the little Post Office on the moor. Lady Chilworth came out of the office as we drove up—in a long waterproof coat, and a little felt hat, with her hair blown about, and her face pale and agitated. Sir George jumped out of the cart as if he had been shot. 'What the devil are you doing up here?' he roared, and then she muttered something—and he called to the groom, 'Drive Mr. Honeybill home; I am walking back with her ladyship.' He looked so savage that I hadn't pluck enough to suggest that her ladyship should drive and I should walk. He'd have bitten my head off, I believe, if I'd chipped in; and so I left them to tramp home together; and I don't envy Lady Chilworth the four mile *tête-à-tête.*"

"Sir George is a fool to make a fuss about nothing. Lady Chilworth has a magnificent constitution, and is fond of walking. She may prefer walking in bad weather to moping in this lonely house—where she has nothing to amuse her."

"Oh, Doctor, you have always a reason for everything she does. Well, she is handsome enough to be forgiven a few eccentricities."

Dr. Rayson walked out of the room without replying.

"Poor old Rayson! Dead nuts on that woman, ain't he?"

"He knew her before her marriage," Halstead answered carelessly, "and no doubt he has a warm regard for her."

"Warmer than I should like, if I were Chilworth."

"Chilworth knows his strength. She adores him."

"And is in a blue funk if he scowls at her. I'd give a good deal to know who and what she was—and the *raison d'être* of the marriage."

"What does it matter? Here we are shooting Chilworth's birds and drinking his wine. We like him pretty well; and we like his house and his moor; we tolerate his cook, and approve his cellar. What does it matter to us if he found his handsome wife on the stage of San Carlos, or picked her out of a Neapolitan gutter?"

"Oh, but it matters intensely to this child. I am devoured with curiosity. It is my mission in life to know everything about everybody."

"Rather a trumpery mission!"

"Altogether trumpery, if you like; but my friends expect it of me. 'Ask Reggie,' they say. 'Reggie is sure to know.' It would be a bad day for Reggie when Reggie didn't know. And I ask you, Halstead, what am I to tell my friends about Lady Chilworth, in the little November season?"

"You must tax your invention."

"That'll be bad for Lady C. You may be sure I shall be much more interesting—and a good deal more improper—than the truth. Five o'clock! I wonder whether Chilworth has come home, and when we are going to have tea."

The second question was answered immediately, by the entrance of the butler.

"Tea is ready in the billiard-room, sir," to Halstead.

"Has your master come in?"

"No, sir. Sir George have not come in."

"Well, we won't keep the teapot waiting. One of my numerous old womanish ways is a liking for a good cup of tea," said Reggie, as he slipped out of the room, followed at a leisurely pace by Henry Halstead.

The gun-room was empty, and the shades of evening closed round the unshuttered windows, that looked across a narrow garden upon the bleak vacancy of the moor. A footman came in presently and swept the hearth, and piled fresh logs upon the waning fire. The rain beat the windows, the wind screamed across the moor. A fitful blaze broke out of the pine logs, and flashed on the shining metal of Chilworth's guns, ranged on the dark brown wall, and on a pair of pistols he was fond of using in an idle hour to show his friends how easy it was for him to hit the pip in a playing card or put out a candle at twenty paces. Whatever George Chilworth cared for doing he contrived to do better than almost anybody else. To excel had been the rule of his life; and if there was any art or business in which he could not be superior he dropped it at once and for ever. Not to be first was intolerable.

The shooting lodge stood in the midst of loneliness, the great rolling moor stretching on one side to the sea, on the other to the dark waste of hills crowned with the rugged crest of massive rock.

The house had begun as a shooter's hut—a place for a couple of men to pig in—and had been expanded gradually in a rough fashion. Chilworth had added this spacious gun-room and a full-sized billiard-room adjoining. The gun-room was furnished with a kind of rough luxury, and served as a family sitting-room.

The gun-room opened directly on the moor. Presently the door was flung open roughly, and Sir George Chilworth came in, threw his deer-stalker cap into a corner, and walked to the fireplace, with quick movements, and the unmistakable air of an angry man. He was followed by his wife, who came slowly to the hearth where he was standing, looking down into the fire, with his back to the room and his folded arms resting on the mantelpiece. He was in shooting clothes, a man of neat, well-knit figure, a little above middle height. His head was small and well-shaped, the dark hair cropped almost as close as a convict's. His face was hidden just now, as he leaned forward, frowning at the fire.

"It is hard that you should be angry with me, George—now—when I am so unhappy."

"Can I help being angry, when you make a fool of yourself, and of me—tramping four miles through the rain, and turning up at the Post Office just as my cart was passing—with that ass Honeybill, too—the most malignant gossip in London?"

"Why do you ask him here if you don't like him?"

"I didn't ask him. He asked himself—and I had to be civil. The little cad is useful, in a way. But that you should give him a handle for tittle-tattle!"

His wife stopped in the act of pulling off her long waterproof cloak, and faced him angrily. She was not one of those slavish wives who submit to be bullied every day of their lives, and kiss the rod, and admire the master who harries them. It had been said that she was afraid of her husband, and it was true that in all small social matters she gave way to him; for she felt herself a stranger in the land, and knew that she was continually erring against those little laws which seemed so trumpery to her, but which were all important to him. But she was a woman of strong feelings, and of an indomitable spirit, and there was a devil within her which it was not well to raise.

If her husband could be angry she could be angry too. Her dark eyes flashed as she faced him, and on the ivory pallor of her cheeks two spots of bright carnation showed suddenly, like danger-signals.

"What do I care for his tittle-tattle—when my darling's life is in danger?"

Chilworth glanced at the billiard-room door, and then went to assure himself that it was properly shut.

"I had waited and waited all the morning for a telegram—waited in an agony of suspense. You don't know what that means, perhaps. You never cared enough about anyone to suffer that kind of agony. But it was more than I could bear—and I think I should have gone mad if I had waited all the afternoon—and no news had come. So I did the best thing I could, which was to walk to Spofforth, and wire an inquiry, and wait there till the answer came."

"And what do you suppose the postmistress thought of your inquiry?"

"There was not much for her to think about. The message was three words—'Is she worse?' I waited an hour and a half for the answer, and this is what came to me."

She handed him a telegram which he read by the firelight. "No improvement—case very serious."

"Poor child!" he sighed. "Well, it is only a childish ailment—which almost every child has to go through. And we know that everything that can be done for her will be done."

"Everything—by strangers, who are paid to take care of her. Everything! and the next message may be that she is dead."

A hoarse sob broke her voice.

"God forbid that it should be so, Mariana, for your sake."

"For my sake! But not for your own. You never, never, never cared for her."

"Her existence was a source of sorrow—for you," he said, in a softer tone, and with some tenderness in his manner. "I could not forget that."

"Shame — humiliation — yes. Her birth brought those—but she—she was my consolation. I lived for her—only for her. She was all the world to me, George—you know she was all the world to me in those lonely years when you were far away and I thought myself deserted and forgotten."

"You had no justification for so thinking."

"Oh, I know you wrote to me from time to time

—a duty-letter. You sent me money which I did not want, for the savings of my prosperous days were enough for our life at Amalfi, in our cottage by the sea. Well—I must not reproach you for those lonely years—since—when your sunshine came—you came back to me—and were generous—generous."

She repeated the adjective in her pretty Italian fashion, and went to him with a sudden impulse of affection, and leaned her head upon his breast.

"Dearest," she said softly, "you made me proud and happy. Never think that I can be ungrateful; but if you would make my life perfect; if you would let our darling live with us—where she has a right to be."

"And let the men who hate me guess the secret of our lives—and turn it against me, and make capital out of it, as they so well know how to do. Morality in England is like a sleeping tiger, Mariana. It wakes whenever a scapegoat is wanted. Remember Sir John Burke—General Vere—Hanway—men of mark in the world of politics—ruined, exiled for one social mistake. We are a scrupulously moral nation when we want to down a man."

"But she might be called my niece."

"An orphan niece! Your living image! Yourself seen through the wrong end of an opera glass. That would be too thin!"

"Well," with a deep-drawn sigh, "you are the master. And now, George, be kind to me. Let me have the carriage to drive me to the station."

"What station?"

"Balmallock. There is an eight o'clock train that will take me to Perth, where I can change to the night express for London."

"Are you mad, Mariana?"

"No, George, perfectly calm and rational. But I must go to London by the night mail, and to Ryde by the first train I can catch. That telegram means danger of death for my child. I should be mad if I did not understand it, mad if I lost one hour in going to her. I may never see her alive, perhaps. The light may have gone out of those sweet eyes before I get to her. But it shall not be my fault if I am too late. It shall not be my fault."

Her voice was broken by sobs—her whole being was shaken by the passion of her grief, as imagination conjured up that fatal end to the child's illness. She pressed the electric bell, keeping her finger upon it till the footman came in.

"Order the station brougham to be got ready immediately; and tell Jessop to put some things into a Gladstone bag—I am going to London for two or three days—and to bring me my carriage cloak, and travelling hat."

"Is Jessop to go with you, my lady?"

"No, no. Give her my message—and be quick about it. Imbecile!" she muttered as the man disappeared, scared by her look and tone.

She had moved away from her husband, and was standing in front of a small glass at the other end of the room. She had taken off her hat, and was arranging her disordered hair with hands that trembled a little.

Sir George came over to her, and laid an angry hand upon her shoulder.

"If you think I shall suffer you to take this mad-headed journey, you must have very little knowledge of my character," he said.

"Oh, I know you, I know," she answered, in her

quick, impassioned way, which made so marked a contrast to his slow, biting accents. "I know you can be as hard as iron when you like—you are proud of your iron will. But I can be hard, too—when my child's life trembles in the balance—when I am going to snatch her last breath—to kiss her dead lips perhaps. I am going to her as fast as the train can carry me."

"You will do nothing of the kind. It is preposterous to think of such a journey—such a scandal. My wife tearing off to London—in this weather—at an hour's notice—alone."

"You can go with me."

"And increase the scandal. You can do no good. I have wired to Mrs. Murray to do everything—to get the highest medical opinion—from London if there is no one good enough in Ryde—to spare neither money nor trouble. What good can we do, you or I? What can the child want that she has not got?"

"Her mother. You don't know what that means—you don't understand the link between mother and child—who have lived together—all in all to each other—for the first four years of that child's existence.

You almost broke her heart when you parted her from me—handed her over to strangers—like a lifeless thing that could know no difference. Oh, God, that I could let her go—that I could be selfish enough to value my advantage—the name and place you gave me—above my child's happiness! But I let her go—and now God is angry with me—and she will die—she will die! Don't try to reason with me, George—you had best let me go quietly."

"Before you make a scene that will disgrace me? I won't let you go—and I won't let you make a scene! You are my wife, Mariana, my wife! I don't think I need remind you that I sacrificed something in order to make crooked things straight. I ran the risk of spoiling my career. You know that, don't you? I depend upon your help—your prudence and tact to further my views in life. I have succeeded so far beyond my hopes—have succeeded at an earlier age than most men—and I have the ball at my feet; but it is in your power to spoil my game. There is a strong influence above the world of politics—a hand that can be lifted to crush a man in the height of success. I don't want to provoke that influence by a senseless scandal—I don't want men going about London telling people that my wife is 'impossible.'"

She stood looking at him with scornful eyes, and a heaving bosom, choking with passion, while he talked to her.

"Honour and conscience—and my affection for you—prompted my conduct. I have no regret for what I did; but I ask for a fair return. I made you my wife, and I must have a wife's obedience. Let me take you to your room—and rest and try to compose yourself between now and dinner. Remember, I cannot have scenes—I cannot have my friends wondering about you."

"If God is good to me, and restores my darling, you shall command my obedience. I will be as submissive as a slave—when I come back. But don't talk of obedience or your friends' opinions to-night—when I have but one thought—how to get to my child. For pity's sake, help me to get away—if you won't come with me."

Lady Chilworth's maid came in with a cloak and hat at this moment, followed by the footman carrying the Gladstone bag. With hurried gestures and in a dead silence Lady Chilworth let the woman dress her for a journey—the long cloth coat, with deep sable collar and cuffs—the neat little felt hat, fitting close to the small head, the doeskin gauntlets—were put on and adjusted.

"That will do. You can go," said her mistress, and then to the footman, "Tell them to make haste with the brougham."

"Yes, my lady."

The two servants disappeared.

George Chilworth walked to the door that opened on the moor, and stood looking at his wife, livid with suppressed rage.

"Well, you have done your worst—made a spectacle of yourself to your servants—created all the talk I wanted to avoid. But if you think you are any nearer carrying out your mad plan by getting a bag packed and ordering a carriage, you are vastly mistaken. You act like a child, Mariana, a pig-headed child, and you must be treated like a child. I tell you plainly that you shall not leave this house to-night."

"And I tell you plainly that nothing short of brute

force will prevent my getting to the station in time for the eight o'clock train. And I suppose you will hardly use that against me."

"I shall use any means that your folly forces me to employ. I will not be defied by my wife."

He stood with his back planted against the door.

"Go to your room and take off those things," he said roughly.

"I am waiting for the carriage. There is plenty of time yet." She looked at the clock on the mantel-piece, and then took out her purse and counted the gold in it, to see if she had enough for her journey, and then stood silent, with her arms folded, looking at Chilworth, in the light of the burning logs.

There was relentless purpose in each face, as wife and husband looked at each other, indomitable resolve, passionate indignation, impatience, despair, a volcano of emotions held in check. They stood thus for some moments that seemed long, while the click of the billiard-balls in the next room—and the dropping of the ashes on the hearth sounded in the silence. Then Mariana began to pace the room—to and fro, with hurried steps, and then she flung herself into a chair, dragged off one loose gauntlet, and sat biting her nails in an agony of nervous impatience, as furiously as if she had been hurting her worst enemy. At the first sound of wheels she sprang to her feet and walked to the door, where George Chilworth was still standing, the image of determination, fixed as fate. He had taken a pipe from his pocket, and filled and lighted it, while she was pacing up and down, and was smoking with an air of quiet enjoyment that intensified her fury.

"The brougham is ready. Let me pass, George."

"My dear Mariana, I have told you that I don't mean to let you go. Come, you have worked off your emotions by this time, I am sure, and you are going to be reasonable."

"Come away from that door," she cried, almost in a scream.

"Not to let you go through it."

"Devil, devil, devil!" she shrieked, "heartless devil! A father, and without a father's feelings—a husband, holding a wife no higher than a bought slave. Will you let me go?"

The brougham was drawn up in the drive outside, and the lamps were shining in the wintry darkness like angry eyes. The click of the balls, the men's voices and laughter sounded from the billiard-room. They were too well amused and occupied to hear those angry voices so near. Chilworth had indeed been careful, even in his angriest moments, to speak in undertones, never forgetting that the ear of the world was near. A man who lives for the world and the world's approval rarely forgets that vicinity. But for the woman's consciousness of listeners they might have been alone in some vast wilderness.

"Your calling me bad names will not make any difference. You may just as well go to your room at once—and get yourself into your right mind. You are only prolonging a painful scene, and making me sorry that I ever asked you to leave a country where the habits and manners of the people suit your own."

He had loved her passionately in his day, but he was so exasperated with her to-night that he took pleasure in wounding her. All thought of their sick child, and of the purpose for which she opposed him, was out of his mind. For him at this moment the struggle meant will against will, temper against temper.

"Come away from that door," she gasped, between

her set teeth, looking about her wildly, till her roaming eyes caught sight of something that fixed them suddenly, in a wide open gaze, half fury, half horror.

Another instant and she had snatched a pistol from the wall—the Colt's revolver that he had been practising with that morning—a dangerous toy in her hands, he thought—for he remembered that he had left some of the chambers charged.

"Come away from that door!" she shrieked, as she raised her arm and took aim at him.

"You hell-cat! do you think I am afraid of——"

He fell, shot through the heart, with the unfinished sentence on his lips.

He had not time to recall the night he first saw her, dressed as a boy, in white from head to foot, shooting at a mark on a music-hall stage, in one of the lowest quarters of Naples.

Exquisitely beautiful, clever, audacious, a child in years, a woman in passion and beauty, able to sing, to act, to dance, to shoot, to fence, the star and chief attraction of a *Café Chantant,* he had seen her, and loved her, and found her irresistible. With all her charm, with all her audacity, he knew himself to be her first lover, and that she could hardly have felt the shame of her surrender more acutely had she been a king's daughter. And then, when unlooked for prosperity came to him, it had seemed so keen a delight to tame this wild bird, to take this child of the people from her vulgar environment, and to train her for a place in the great world—the world he worshipped. The scheme might have answered better, perhaps, with a different trainer, but George Chilworth's hand upon the curb had been too heavy, and this is how it ended.

CHAPTER I.

THE placid close of an exquisite day; the peaceful evening of a prosperous life; the scene a villa garden on the shore of Lake Como, a long terrace shaded by spreading planes, willows dipping in the water, and across the lake, dazzling in the sunlight, the white walls and tall cupola of Bellagio, the pink and yellow houses, the green blinds, the striped awnings, the red roofs, a medley of colour dimly defined in the distance, and, crowning all, the wooded crest of the hill where the Villa Serbaloni smiles at the westering sun. The personages, Sir William Rayson, the famous physician, his daughter Rosamund, his widowed sister, Mrs. Dalrymple, and her daughter, Octavia.

Time had silvered William Rayson's head since that night of horror in a Scotch shooting lodge, which stood out from the background of commonplace memories with an appalling distinctness, a group of figures lit with lurid light, and isolated on the edge of a storm-dark horizon. There are tragedies in life that a man of deep feeling cannot forget, albeit he may have played only a subordinate part in the catastrophe, may have been indeed little more than a looker on.

At the time of Sir George Chilworth's untimely end, William Rayson had been in the prime of middle-life, a man who had already made his mark in West End London as a consulting physician, and whose waiting-rooms in Cavendish Place were always full. Some years later, Sir William Rayson, baronet, had become the one man to whom all fashionable London flocked. He was the universal healer, the nerve-doctor, the friend and adviser, the last hope of the despairing, the sustainer of the weak, the modern Alcides for ever wrestling with the enemy of man.

And to-day, fifteen years after the tragedy on the moor between Spofforth and Balmallock, Sir William Rayson was spending the evening of life in retired leisure, having worked as few men work, and succeeded as few men succeed, and being content to leave the arena to his younger competitors, and to those of his contemporaries who did not know when to say *Opus operandum est.*

This eventide of life was full of sweetness for him—he had his daughter and only child, his constant companion, the idol of his great warm heart. His eager mind found interest and occupation in the progress of medical science. His pen found employment, and his influence was still a living thing in the medical world. He had no sense of being superseded, though another man sat in the spacious consulting-room in Cavendish Place. He was resting from the long life-toil; but he was not idle, and he was never bored.

He had made a handsome fortune, as fortunes go among professional men. Measured by their standard he was rich; though from a diamond-merchant's or newspaper-proprietor's point of view his income would but rank as respectable poverty. He owned this villa at Tremezzo, built with reckless outlay, bought for less than half its cost from the executors of an Italian prima donna. He had a Georgian Manor House near Hampton-on-Thames, where he lived during the greater part of the year, and where he dispensed a judicious hospitality. Sir William Rayson's Sunday luncheons and dinners were among the most popular entertainments of the London season.

In England or in Italy the guiding star of Sir William's life was his daughter, Rosamund, who had been his dearest companion ever since she could remember, from the old days in Cavendish Place—where she used to sit and prattle to him while he ate his solitary dinner after the long toilsome day, a child in a white frock and blue sash, with a sage black poodle sitting by her side—to this present time when she was of an age to take an intelligent interest in almost every subject that interested him, even to the latest discovery in medical science.

In all those years she had lived in his sight and in his constant care. She had been educated at home, by a German governess, a woman of strong common-sense, and an accomplished musician, and thus capable of developing Rosamund's musical talent, which was of a high order. But while Fräulein Ascher taught her pupil all that a well-brought-up young lady is expected to know, there was another education of a wider reach going on from day to day in Rosamund's intimate association with her father, one of the cleverest men of his generation. It was in those happy evening hours, between Sir William's eight o'clock dinner and Rosamund's ten o'clock bedtime, that the young mind took its strongest growth, unconsciously absorbing the physician's ideas upon men and things, upon art and manners, politics and literature. From the time she was old enough to think grave thoughts he had treated her as a companion and friend, and had talked with her as if they two—the girl in her teens and the mature *savant*—had been upon an intellectual equality.

He had taken care that while her mind expanded her physique was not neglected. He gave her friends and playfellows of her own age. She danced and rode, and played tennis and golf. Life had been full of delight for her, from the hour she became conscious of her father's existence, and could recall that noble head, iron-grey as she first remembered it, white as it was now, a leonine head, a commanding countenance, with wide forehead, great breadth between the eyes, brows strongly marked and bushy, the nose broad and straight, the nose of a Jupiter rather than an Apollo, mouth mobile and capable of extremes of tenderness and severity—lips that in desperate moments when the man's mind was resolved and the stake was a life, seemed carved out of marble.

Sometimes, in an hour of pensive reverie, Rosamund looked back along that flowery pathway of her joyous girlhood and called up the pictures of the past. In all of them her father was the principal figure; under Providence the giver of all good. But her memory did not carry her as far back as she desired. She had girl-friends who could recall events that had happened before their third birthday—who could remember themselves toddling and tumbling about sunny lawns—scrambling into their mothers' laps, riding in donkey-panniers—nursing idolised kittens—in the dim dawn of reason. But to her it seemed as if a heavy cloud had spread itself over the scene of her childhood. In vain did she try to evoke the image of her father amidst those faint shadows which made up her childish memories: the bright blue sea, smiling under perpetual sunshine; a life that seemed all sunlight and sweet warm air, and rainbow hued shells which she played with all day long, sitting on a stretch of golden sands set like a jewel in a crescent of grey rocks, which changed to crimson and purple and orange when the low sun touched them, and when sky, and sea, and shore were all transfigured with an overpowering brilliancy of colour and light.

This scene flashed through the dark clouds that veiled her infant memories, and with the scene came the memory of a voice that sang to her, lips that kissed her, a woman's face that smiled upon her, but over all there hung the same cloud, and she could neither recall the features of that ever-present face, nor tell whether it was mother or nurse who had guarded and cherished her beside that sunlit sea, nor could she conjure up any distinct picture of the house she had lived in. She knew only that a change came over the scene, from heat to cold, from colour to greyness. It was the sea still, but a different sea, and she wondered whether it was but the change from summer to winter, or whether her faint and confused memories of dust, and heat, and weariness, were memories of a journey that had lasted many days. Mixed with the vision of that grey sea and colder sky came the sound of strange voices, and then she remembered her father's iron-grey head bending over the sofa where she lay, no longer caring for toys or sea-weed or flowers, but feeling tired, very tired, all day long. The sea was near her still—the blue expanse stretched itself opposite an open window, and one day her father's strong arms lifted her off her sofa, and carried her out upon the golden sands, where she found the bright-hued sea-weeds she loved, and shells, too, but not so many as in her older memories.

But from this hour the pictures of the past came out of the cloud, and grew distinct and vivid as the scenes of yesterday: the blunt features of her homely nursery governess, a German, like that more accomplished woman who had educated her; the school-room in Cavendish Place with its flower-pots, and gay pictures, and striped Spanish blinds, and pretty bamboo furniture, all colour and brightness, and its inexhaustible toy-closet, and rich supply of picture books; and above all, and better than all, her father's delightful companionship, her father's explanation of the pictures in the books, by which the foundations of general knowledge were laid, from the stripes on the zebra's coat to the wonders of the starry heavens.

Her mother must have died, she thought, during that dark interval in which the background of her life had shifted. Once, and once only, when she was between nine and ten years old, she had questioned her father about that missing face; but child as she was, his look of mental pain had so impressed her that she never again approached the subject. A child, brought up in constant association with a man of mature age, would naturally have tact beyond that of average children.

She questioned the Fräulein, who could tell her nothing of the past, except that Madame Rayson must have died more than a year before she, the Fräulein, had entered upon her duties at Cavendish Place, since Rosa was then out of mourning. Rosa had to be told the meaning of the word mourning, in that sense; but she could not remember having ever worn black frocks and everything black like those children Fräulein pointed out in the Park where they were walking when the explanation was made.

That dismal black raiment was among the many things lost in the cloud that veiled Rosamund's childhood.

And now Rosamund was grown up. She was no longer everybody's Rosa, a pet and plaything, flitting about as freely as the birds and butterflies. She was Miss Rayson, only child and heiress of Sir William Rayson, a young lady who required a chaperon, a fact which fell out greatly to the advantage of Sir William's sister, Mrs. Dalrymple, a widow with an only daughter and an only son, the latter the apple of her eye, recently called to the Bar, but as yet briefless.

This little family had until lately occupied somewhat exiguous lodgings in Upper Delafield Place, which is to Delafield Place proper as moonlight is to sunlight, and as water is to wine. The great gulf of the Marylebone Road makes all the difference between Philistine prosperity, an address that nobody need blush for, and shabby gentility, an address that everybody would like to hide. Heavens, how the drawing-room windows and balconies and street doors dwindle and shrink when the explorer has crossed the road from Delafield to Upper Delafield! What vulgar brass plates of dressmakers, pianoforte-tuners, water-rate collectors, replace the physician's honoured name, or the "Ring also" of respectability. How Wilfred Dalrymple hated that shabby first-floor parlour, misnamed drawing-room, in which they lived and ate—a room where mixed odours of dust and meals were not to be driven away. More than once Wilfred had conjured his mother to take a house, and furnish it ever so humbly, rather than submit to the misery of lodgings.

"It would be our own, and it would be clean," he said, "no matter what it was like in other respects."

"Wilfred, have you ever calculated the cost of a house?" Mrs. Dalrymple inquired solemnly, and on her son's confessing himself without ideas upon the subject she ran over an appalling list of items—furniture, rent, taxes, rates, insurance, gas, repairs, breakages, servants, till he cried, "Hold, enough," and submitted to the inevitable.

"With a small fixed income like mine the only true economy is to have no settled home. If we were to find these rooms too dear, we could get cheaper rooms at Notting Hill"—Wilfred shuddered perceptibly—"but this is a good address."

"Upper Delafield Place? Well, the address is better than the street perhaps—but not much, not much."

"You see, with an income like mine there is no margin," continued his mother. "Suppose I were foolish enough to take a house—which I could only do by buying furniture on the three-years system."

"Oh, don't, don't talk about it!" groaned Wilfred. "Why did God make a beautiful world to populate it with paupers? Think of the houses in Park Lane—the villas along the Riviera—and that we who have taste and education must live among such furniture as this," with a malignant kick at a cheap walnut-wood chair upholstered in grass-green rep; "or buy a few wretched sticks on the three-years system."

"And if we had our own house and furniture, the bursting of a kitchen boiler would cripple me for a year," resumed Mrs. Dalrymple, who was accustomed to her son's vehemence.

He was a good son, kind and forbearing, and his outbreaks of rebellion against Fate never meant ill temper towards his mother.

"Besides," pursued Mrs. Dalrymple, "while we are in lodgings we are perfectly independent, and one never knows what may happen."

"True! But the unexpected thing that happens is generally something unpleasant," said Wilfred, and then he took up the thick imperial octavo that lay on the shabby carpet beside his rickety armchair, and tried to concentrate his faculties upon Stubbs on "Contingent Remainders."

He was a hard-working young man, had done well at a modern Oxford College which he never cared to mention, and was now reading hard, after a year in a well-known barrister's chambers. He had a third share in two rooms on a fourth floor in Pump Court; but squalid as were the Upper Delafield Place lodgings, he preferred the privacy of home to the rowdy companionship of his co-tenants.

This time the unexpected was a stroke of fortune Mrs. Dalrymple had never dared to hope for, though she hoped much from a wealthy brother with an only child. From the day when her husband, a Major in a line regiment, had died and left her with a widow's pension, and the income provided by her marriage settlement, William Rayson had been her strong rock. Her means just sufficed for the needs of daily life—lodgings, food, clothes and an occasional doctor's bill, generally rendered in a mitigated form to so near a relative of the great physician—but there had been no margin for education, and it was Sir William who had paid Wilfred's Oxford expenses and Temple fees, and his niece Octavia's bills at a convent at Bruges, where she was received as a pupil in spite of the difference of creed.

Mrs. Dalrymple was in the habit of telling her son

and daughter that there never was a better uncle than their uncle; but until the last two years she had been forced to admit that his benefactions seemed to be prompted by a strict sense of duty rather than a warm affection for his relations, since he had seen very little of his sister after her marriage, and had allowed his nephew and niece to grow up almost as strangers to him and his daughter.

This, to Mrs. Dalrymple, a weak, fond woman, who adored her children, was an unpardonable affront. Within the last year he had suddenly changed his tactics and had invited his sister and daughter to take up their abode under his roof for an indefinite period, as Rosamund's chaperon and companion, "as long as the arrangement works comfortably for us all," he wrote; and Mrs. Dalrymple gave her landlord notice without an hour's delay, exulting at her own wisdom in not having encumbered herself with a house full of furniture.

Wilfred was to find residential chambers in the Temple, a luxury that could now be afforded, and a delightful prospect after Upper Delafield Place. The circumstances of the little family had been altered in an hour, and Mrs. Dalrymple could now lavish her small means upon the son she worshipped, instead of having to deny him every privilege of young manhood. Nor was she long without far-reaching thoughts of the brilliant future that opened before him. Once admitted to a cousinly intimacy with Sir William's heiress, what more likely than that they should fall in love with each other? Wilfred was clever and handsome, full of ambition and working power. His uncle must needs appreciate his talents and industry, and could hardly object to him as a suitor.

And now in this delicious autumn weather, in this bright expanse of garden between mountain and lake, the cousins were sharing in pleasures that were all new to Wilfred and Octavia, who had hitherto known life only on its rougher side, the perpetual struggle for bread and gentility, the unrelenting effort to make ends meet. Ends met easily now, and lapped over, for the income which was so tight a fit for a family of three made an ample provision for a bachelor in Temple Chambers, while Wilfred had already begun to feel the effect of his uncle's influence in the shape of briefs from solicitors of position in the great world, men who honoured William Rayson, and were glad to help his nephew.

Afternoon tea had been done with an hour ago, but one little Japanese tea-table had been left in a sheltered corner by a standard magnolia, with all things ready for a late comer. A visitor was expected by the evening boat from Como, the son of Sir William's old friend, Sir Henry Halstead, lately raised to the Bench, after a prosperous career at the Bar.

Mrs. Dalrymple appeared keenly interested in the expected guest. "You have told me so little about him, Rosa," she said, almost querulously, when her niece seated herself on the low garden bench beside her Aunt's Trouville chair after a set at tennis with Wilfred.

"I don't know what more there is to tell, auntie. You ask if he is handsome? I reply, no. If he is ugly? I answer, *C'est selon.* My maid says yes. Has he fascinating manners to atone for a plain face? Well, I really can't apply the word fascinating to any male creature. But if you ask me if Ronald Halstead is all I like a young man to be, I answer, 'Yes—yes-issimo!'"

"I understand he was almost a son of the house of Tangley."

"Almost, though he did not come there often. You see, Sir Henry Halstead is my father's oldest friend, so it was natural that father should like Sir Henry's only son. It seemed an odd coincidence that father should have an only daughter, and his friend an only son—but Ronald is luckier than I, for he has a mother who idolises him, and would be a perfect mother if she were not so dreadfully fat that I think he must sometimes find himself blushing for her—when he has to introduce his 'Varsity pals to so much mother. But then Ronald is an adorable son, and he goes to parties with Lady Halstead night after night, and sees her wedged in doorways, and entangled in masses of humanity, and never lets on that he thinks there's a superfluous ounce of her."

"'Lets on' is a vulgar expression, Rosa dearest."

"Oh, I know. I got it from Wilfred. Those vulgar phrases come so handy."

"And as to any young man or woman being luckier than you, Rosa, the mere suggestion of such a thing on your part seems like flying in the face of Providence.

Never was a girl more happily placed, never was there a kinder father."

"Ah, auntie, tell me that Italian skies are blue, and that Italian lakes are deep, tell me that two-and-two make four—by way of a novelty. As if I did not know that I have fed on the roses and lain in the lilies of life! As if I did not know that my darling father is the most perfect of men and parents! I do know, and I thank God for my happy life, night and morning, in a thanksgiving that always seems new. But still I can't help thinking it must be nice to have a mother as well as a father."

"Your friend Ronald appears to have been somewhat indifferent to both parents, as he has preferred going after big game in the Himalayas to staying at home with his people."

"Perhaps he is rather too restless a spirit. He loves sport and adventure. He went in for athletics at the 'Varsity, was in the Cambridge eleven, and I'm afraid he took the very poorest thing in honours, just scraped through. But he is very clever, all the same, auntie, as you'll discover when he has been with us a day or two; and he is just as good as he is clever."

"If he is really clever it seems extraordinary that he should have been allowed to grow up without a profession. I wonder Sir Henry did not want his son to follow in his own footsteps."

"That's because you don't know Sir Henry. My father and he are ideal parents. Sir Henry declares he would never have his son waste the best years of his life in slaving at the Bar, in order to make a fortune that he could do without, and a name that would be forgotten in the next generation. 'I have worked hard enough to afford myself the luxury of an idle son.' That's what I've heard Sir Henry tell people when they bothered him about Ronald's career—and wondered, as you wonder, why the poor creature was allowed to enjoy himself."

"A life of idleness is not a good life for any man," sighed Mrs. Dalrymple.

"Idleness! Why, Ronald is the most industrious young man I know. From the days when he was a dry Bob at Eton to this very week, which he has been spending on wheels between Brindisi and Como, I don't believe he has ever known what it is to be idle. His highest idea of rest is making trout flies or cleaning his bicycle. And if you knew the Alpine climbing he has done, the enormous aprons of ice he has crossed—where to shout to a comrade might be to loosen an avalanche, and send himself and his party to a bottomless abyss. Look, the steamer, and now you will see the idle young man."

She sprang up from her low chair, and ran to her father, who was playing chess with his niece at the other end of the terrace.

"Father, the steamer is close, close; and Ronald will be here in a few minutes. I am so glad! After two years! It was two years last Wednesday since he sailed for Bombay—two years! Two years' roughing it in the Himalayas, or tramping about Cashmere. What a barbarian, what a sunburnt savage he must have grown!"

The steamer was nearer, and out of sight, in the little port round the corner. Rosamund ran to the house to order tea in no dainty Japanese half-pint teapot, but a big silver pot of tea. Tea as for a son of Anak. She knew her hunter's habits and ways.

Sir William and Octavia rose from the chess table. Wilfred shut his book, and got up from the grass where he had been lying. Mrs. Dalrymple put away her knitting in the big satin bag which accompanied her everywhere: the bag which in the days of her poverty had held the family stockings, and had to be hidden when visitors were expected, but which now contained only such work as a lady may freely leave about her sitting-room. Everybody was eagerly expectant.

Five minutes, ten minutes, and then a tall, broad-shouldered figure in a light grey cycling suit appeared at a bend of the garden, wheeling a bicycle, which at sight of the group on the terrace he shoved hastily into a bush, and came running to greet his friends.

"My dear Sir William, how do you do? How fit, how uncommonly fit you are looking! Time moves backward for good people. And Rosa—time has gone the other way for you. You've grown half a head taller. You used to be as high as my heart, but now you are nearly as high as my head."

"Let me introduce you to my sister and niece,

before you begin to tease Rosa. Mr. Halstead, Mrs. Dalrymple, Miss Dalrymple—and my nephew Wilfred."

The new-comer smiled a broad, frank smile, and offered his hand freely, with an air of being sure that everybody was glad to see him.

"She need not have hesitated about calling him ugly," thought Mrs. Dalrymple, "but I suppose he has what people call a distinguished air."

Octavia thought him ugly but magnificent, a man whom everybody would recognise at a glance as a "personage."

He was six feet two, with broad shoulders, narrow hips, the long lean arms of an athlete, the strong muscular legs of a runner. His dark complexion had been dyed almost to copper colour by sun and wind and rain and snow—a long experience of all that is roughest in the atmosphere. His eyes, dark grey eyes, well opened, quick of glance and changeful of expression, were his best feature, and he had a fine set of teeth. For the rest his face was somewhat roughly moulded, and would have attracted a painter's eye by its strong character, but never by its beauty. The contrast between this wandering athlete and Wilfred Dalrymple, the man of streets and law courts, was curiously marked. Dalrymple was eminently handsome, but he had all the characteristics of a dweller in cities; slender of frame, of pale complexion, and thoughtful countenance, the delicate outline of nose and cheek and chin more attenuated than was natural to youth—a face which showed signs of suffering as well as of thought.

His mother's watchful eye glanced complacently from the rough-hewn features of the new-comer to her son's classic profile. "Not much fear of rivalry there," she thought.

But Octavia, whose ideas were essentially modern, took a different view of the case.

"The man is just ugly enough to be irresistible to such a girl as Rosamund," she told herself.

CHAPTER II.

THERE could hardly have been a livelier household all along Como's lovely shores than that of the Villa Viola after the coming of Ronald Halstead. They had been very happy before his arrival, but with a passive happiness, the idly contemplative attitude of mind, the *dolce fa* which after a time conduces to boredom, a satiety of sweetness, too much blue in the sky and on the lake, too many heavily scented flowers, an overpowering perfume, too much music on the water, too much leisure for memories and regrets.

But with Ronald's coming life changed and was all action. He had the two girls out on the lake at seven o'clock on the morning after his arrival, rowed them to Varenna and gave them breakfast in a cottage on the edge of the water, where they ate peasant's fare with more gusto than the refined *déjeuner* of the villa. He organised long rambles in upland meadows above Bellagio, flower and fern hunts, in which he taught them more botany than they had ever learnt in the school-room, for without being a student of books this young man had an avidity for all knowledge and went through the world picking up facts and fancies, and storing them in a capacious memory. He organised cycling expeditions along the margin of the lake, wherever a cycle could travel, shipping cycles and riders in one of the broad bottomed country boats when the road was impossible.

And then there was tennis or croquet, the latter being almost the only form of rest which these eager young people allowed themselves. For Wilfred, who had led a consistent indoor life ever since he left the 'Varsity, this unrelenting activity was a severe ordeal, but his power of endurance was greater than his physical strength, and he gave himself no respite from these strenuous pleasures. Not for worlds would he have suffered Rosamund to think of him as "a poor creature."

Sir William heard of their expeditions and adventures with pleasure, sometimes accompanying them in a long afternoon drive, but for the most part spending his days in studious restfulness, reading or writing in an open pavilion on the terrace, or pacing slowly up and down the perfumed shrubberies in quiet contemplation. These days of leisure after long years of work were full of placid enjoyment for the man who was as much a student at sixty-five as he had been at twenty. His eager mind followed every advance in the world's education, every development in the various branches of science, and there was scarcely a day that did not afford some new point of interest for the all-round student and thinker.

But stronger than this white light of intellect, glowed the warm red light of love. His daughter's affection was more to him than all the inventions and discoveries of men; his daughter's happiness was the supreme desire of his life. He had made her all that seemed to him good in woman, his ideal woman. He meant to leave her rich—but he had to contemplate that inevitable parting, and those future years in which she must depend on other protection than his, and his most ardent desire was to see her happily married to a good man.

It was not without thought that he had allowed his only sister's son to enter into Rosamund's life. He had kept his kindred at arm's length for a long time, having his own motives for that aloofness, but there had come a time when his fine sense of duty urged him to be something more than a distant benefactor to his sister's children. He had other considerations also, for he told himself that his sister's son, of whom he had heard nothing but praise, might be a good husband for Rosamund were he able to win her heart.

"I'll give the fellow a chance," he resolved, after long deliberation. "My darling does not know what a lover's love means, and he will have fifty to one in his favour as her first admirer. Blood is thicker than water —I ought to give Wilfred a chance, for his mother's sake. He is the paragon of young men for her; and it would be hard lines if I kept him at a distance now that Rosa is grown up, and that I have made her position as my heiress incontestable."

This decision had been arrived at early in the present year, and Wilfred had been a frequent visitor at Tangley Manor, where his mother and sister were installed as residents. But although Rosamund welcomed her aunt and cousins, and liked them all, Sir William had so far discovered no sign of anything warmer than liking on her side. On Wilfred's part he suspected a deeper feeling, and since Ronald's appearance on the scene the physician's keen eye had noted indications of a lover's jealous watchfulness, and he was disposed to regret that he had replied so hospitably to Ronald's telegram from Brindisi, asking if he might take the villa on his way home. The answer had been: "Come, and stay as long as you can," and Ronald had announced his intention of stopping till they all left Italy in October.

"Or Dalrymple and I could start a week in advance and cycle from Lucerne to Calais," he suggested, to which Wilfred replied:

"I had rather carry my cousin's dressing-bag—which weighs about a hundredweight—at every change on the journey, than run the risk of a burst tyre thirty miles from anywhere."

"My dear fellow, if you think of risks you are no cyclist," answered the other.

Sir William was sorry he had invited this early friend of Rosamund's, although he seemed an unlikely competitor against an attractive young man like Wilfred.

But in his heart of hearts Sir William liked his old friend's son better than his own nephew.

"Blood is thicker than water," he repeated to himself, pacing the terrace in the drowsy warmth of afternoon, when the fragrance of the olea filled the air. "I shouldn't like young Halstead to stand in Wilfred's way—but I don't think there can be much fear of him. The very fact that he and Rosa were boy and girl together is against him. A girl seldom cares for an old playfellow."

The footman was setting out the tea tables in the favourite spot by the marble steps that led down to the lake, while Mrs. Dalrymple sat in her Trouville chair, nodding occasionally in an afternoon doze, with her knitting on her lap. Her brother's eyes glanced at her suddenly as he passed her chair.

"Poor old Margaret! It is something to have rescued her from the martyrdom of shabby gentility," he thought. "Those wretched lodgings of hers weighed heavily upon my conscience. Only we two in the world, and one rich and the other poor! Heaven must frown upon such an anomaly."

He stopped near the steps to watch the approach

of the family boat, the red caps of the two boatmen, the scarlet and apple-green umbrellas of the two girls lighted to dazzling brightness by the sunshine.

The two young men were there, one at the rudder, the other lying in the prow, both in white from head to foot, but Sir William was surprised to see a third figure on the cushioned seat next Rosamund, a small man in a grey suit, who took off his straw hat and waved it in an effusive salutation as the boat neared the steps.

"It's that prying little gossip, Honeybill," muttered Sir William, turning suddenly and walking away, with an air of inexpressible annoyance. "What the devil brings him here?"

The young people came trooping up the marble stairs, full of talk and laughter, Honeybill's shrill little reed sounding above all deeper tones, in the concluding sentence of an ill-natured anecdote.

Rosamund ran after Sir William, and gave him one of her childish hugs. It was so difficult for a petted daughter who had never left her father's side to preserve the line of demarcation between child and woman.

"We have brought a strange man to tea, father," she said gaily, "a little man with a squeaky voice. Wilfred calls him Reggie. A funny little man who swears he knows you intimately."

"Yes, I know Mr. Honeybill, but it is a good many years since I met him."

"And you didn't want to meet him again," said Rosa, quick to read the thought behind his speech. "I'm so sorry we brought him to tea."

"You needn't be sorry, dear. He would have come without bringing. Well, we must make the best of him."

"Wilfred thinks him so amusing."

"Wilfred would. One must be very young to appreciate Honeybill."

They sauntered to the spot where Mrs. Dalrymple was pouring out tea in the midst of an archipelago of little tables—olive wood, bamboo, wicker-work—on which fluttered daintiest tea-cloths of muslin, silk, lace, frilled, embroidered, insertioned, hemstitched—the trivial prettiness that marks a house where a girl is mistress. Sir William shook hands with Honeybill, but not cordially, and sank with a tired air into his favourite armchair, and took his cup of tea from his daughter's hand in silence, while the visitor hung over the tea-tray and made himself agreeable to Mrs. Dalrymple. He seemed so pleased with the lady's society, that he lingered at her side after tea was over, and the young people had gone off to the tennis court, and Sir William had taken up his book and retired to his temple of silence at the further end of the terrace.

"It was a surprise to tumble against your son in one of those steep smelly little lanes at Varenna," he said to Mrs. Dalrymple. "He and I are old pals, don't you know."

"I have often heard him talk of you, and your amusing stories. You are a member of his club, I think."

"The Latehours? Yes, I too have been in Arcadia. What a delicious girl your niece is! I never saw a lovelier face—but a little foreign, don't you know. That magnificent black hair, and those superb eyes suggest the sunny South. Was her mother an English woman?"

"I never heard to the contrary." Honeybill looked

surprised. "You see I was with my husband in India when my brother married, and William was never a good correspondent; and when I came home he had been a widower for some years, and I dared not talk to him about his marriage. He has one of those self-contained natures for which a great grief means a great silence."

"To me it was a surprise to find Sir William with a grown-up daughter," said Honeybill, "for I was shooting in Scotland with him fifteen years ago, and it was my impression then, and I believe everybody else's impression, that he was a confirmed bachelor."

He kept his keen and bird-like eye upon Mrs. Dalrymple's face as he talked, ready to take the first warning of displeasure, but he only saw an eager desire to hear more.

"I take it there must have been a touch of romance in his marriage," he said.

"You mean perhaps that he married beneath him?"

"Well, the romantic marriage is apt to take that line—especially when a man keeps the wife in the background, and allows himself to be thought a bachelor."

"My brother has always been reticent about his own affairs," said Mrs. Dalrymple; "but he has been especially so about his married life—though I gather that he was devotedly attached to Rosamund's mother."

"To Rosamund's mother—yes—no doubt," said Honeybill, with a curious inward smile.

"He has been silent, and I have respected his silence. He is as good a brother and uncle as he is a father—better, perhaps, for he does not spoil me or my daughter as he spoils Rosamund."

"Does he spoil that lovely girl? Yes, of course, he would. She has all the charm of a spoilt child—frank, impetuous, impulsive, a little wilful. Well, Sir William Rayson is one of the most advanced spirits of an advanced age, and you have reason to be proud of him and of his career. When I think of the distinguished lives he has prolonged to the last attenuated thread of existence—when I think of the strong men he has plucked from the jaws of death! A great physician, Mrs. Dalrymple, is the modern Alcides."

She thought he meant Æsculapius, but she passed over the error with a bland smile.

"I have always been proud of my brother," she

said. "Was it at the Duke of Netherland's Castle you met him—I know he used to go there for the deer stalking?"

"No, it was on a grouse moor in Argyllshire, with Sir George Chilworth. Halstead's father was there at the same time. It was a visit for ever memorable to all of us, for it ended prematurely in the murder of our host."

"Chilworth—yes, I remember the case. His wife shot him in a fit of madness, and my brother gave evidence in her favour—as to her state of mind, I mean. We were at a hill station where there were very few English, but I know there was quite a struggle for the newspapers with the report of the trial. My husband had met Sir George Chilworth in London. What became of the wretched woman?"

"She was remitted to a lunatic asylum, during Her Majesty's pleasure."

"Poor wretch! And is she still living?"

"I have not heard of her death."

"You were there? You knew her?"

"Yes. I ate my breakfast with her on the morning before the murder. We were talking and laughing about the Argyllshire cook's scones and baps—and the Argyllshire footman's lingo."

"Was she a very dreadful person?"

"The handsomest brunette I ever saw—with the exception of your niece."

"Oh, please don't mention my niece in the same breath with that horrible woman. She was a singing girl at a music hall in the slums of Naples, was she not?"

"Something of that kind. Her antecedents were raked up at the trial. Poor Chilworth! He had tried to pass her off as a lady, and I believe he had suffered agonies of apprehension lest her history should crop up, and disgrace him. He was the very last man to make a low marriage—a man with an aching self-consciousness, and an inordinate ambition. Poor wretch, what a hell his grave would have been for him if he had known the revelations at the trial."

"Do you think she was mad when she killed him?"

"We have Sir William's evidence upon that fact."

"My brother may have strained a point to save her life."

"Sir William! On oath? Impossible."

"No, no, of course not. He would not perjure himself, even to save a life——"

"Not even to save a woman he greatly admired."

"His admiration could not have amounted to much."

"Indeed! But why not?"

"You forget that my brother was then a married man."

"True, my dear lady. But a married man is human, and a husband who for his own reasons keeps his wife in the background may occasionally forget that he has a wife. He lives two lives, you see—and in the bachelor phase is free to admire a beautiful woman —with enthusiasm."

"William is a man of the highest principles, Mr. Honeybill."

"I submit to your reproof, Mrs. Dalrymple, though I didn't deserve it. I am second to none in my admiration for Sir William Rayson. Shall we go and watch the tennis? Your daughter looks like a fine player."

Mrs. Dalrymple simpered at this inferential praise

of Octavia's slight and supple figure. She knew that in beauty, her daughter and Rosamund were not on the same plane—but Octavia was good-looking enough to pass as handsome in a picture hat, and her figure, from the fashion-plate point of view, was perfection.

Mr. Honeybill was charmed with the performance of the four players—Rosamund and Wilfred against Ronald, heavily handicapped, and Octavia, who had played daily among the "children" at her convent, and was only a little inferior to her cousin—and his interest in the match was keen enough to keep him on the ground, till the players were fain to stop for want of light, and then, no one having asked him to dinner, he wished everybody good night, and went off to catch the steamer for Bellagio, promising to look them up early next day.

He had discovered that neither Wilfred nor his sister had seen the Villa Carlotta, and he had insisted upon being their cicerone for the garden and the Thorwaldsen frieze. Rosamund professed herself satiated with the beauties of the Villa.

"You see I have had to take so many friends over

it," she said, "and I really forgot that my cousins might think it worth seeing."

"Well, is your visitor gone?" Sir William asked his daughter, when she went to look for him in his study, never being able to endure life long away from him.

"Yes, he is gone at last. He stuck, and stuck, and stuck—*ecco quel seccatore!* And he promises to come back early to-morrow, to take Octavia and Wilfred over the Villa Carlotta. He seems rather struck with Octavia. What is he, father?"

"He is one of a large band of diners-out who can be invited within three days of a dinner-party. He has neither birth, money, nor brains, but his conversation is considered delightful."

"But how can that be?"

"He is a preliminary speaking tube, and conveys jokes and scandals from table to table. He keeps the best sayings of other people in perpetual circulation, and ranks as a wit this evening on the strength of a joke he heard yesterday."

"A plagiarist?"

"No, my dear, for he always prefaces his story with,

'What do you think the Dean of Chatham said yesterday?' Or, 'Have you heard Lord Rodobury's last?' And then he sets everybody laughing, and his hostess is delighted."

"Then he is not rich enough to marry Octavia?"

"No, my little matchmaker. And he is a bachelor by profession, with a lump of Nesselrode pudding in the place where some men have hearts."

"What a prejudiced old person you are," she cried, laughing at him, "and your prejudices infect other people. Ronald and I hate Mr. Honeybill already."

"Go on hating him, Rosa. I don't want him on these premises. And now go and dress for dinner—and leave me to seal my letters."

He kissed her, and put her out of the room; then lighted the taper in the silver stand by his desk, and left it burning, and the letter lying unsealed, while he paced the room slowly, with bent head, as he had paced his consulting-room in Cavendish Place sometimes when he was troubled about a case.

"A cloud no bigger than a man's hand," he mused. "It is only a little cloud, but it makes a dark spot in a sky where all was fair."

CHAPTER III.

THE happy days went by, and it was only the shortening of those golden afternoons that ever awakened Rosamund to the consciousness of Time's flight. She shivered when she thought of the coming winter and the change from this radiant shore to the garden at Tangley Manor, where only chrysanthemums and belated dahlias would enliven the autumnal greyness. But the thought that sometimes dashed her joy was not so much the idea of leaving this Italian paradise, which she always left with regret, as the prospect of parting with Ronald Halstead, that energetic traveller having announced his intention of starting on an Australasian tour in the coming November, a tour that would occupy at least a year, and might spin itself out much longer if he did the Pacific Islands, and came home by California and New York.

The Italian weather was perfect. The days and nights were balmy, though the mountains were crested with snow, and September was nearly over. It was still weather for open-air tea-parties on the hill above Lecco, or in the gardens of the Serbaloni Villa, still delicious weather for idling on the lake where Ronald and Wilfred had superseded Sir William's Italian boatmen, who did not eat the bread of idleness, as they were also house-servants, doing all a footman's duties, under the direction of a despotic English butler who had been in the physician's service for a quarter of a century.

Ronald abandoned his idea of riding his bicycle from Lucerne to Calais, and it was he, for the most part, who carried Rosamund's travelling bag, willing as her cousin was to attend upon her. Indeed, if Wilfred had been inclined at any time to forgetfulness, he had his mother ever on the alert to remind him of his duty—an alertness which irritated her son beyond measure.

"I should take it as a favour if you'd treat me less like a performing poodle, mother," he said querulously, "and not remind me at every station that I have Rosamund and her wraps and bags to look after. You weary me and her by all that fuss."

"You have such a casual air, sometimes, Wilfred; and when I remember how much you owe your uncle——"

"You'll make me detest my uncle, if you go on strumming on that note, mother. No man loves a creditor he can't pay. I wish you'd let me accept Sir William's bounties as freely as he gives them, and forget that there's any obligation on my side."

"That's all very well, dear; and indeed I know how sensitive you are."

"Sensitive be hanged! I hate such woman's words applied to me. I'm not what you call sensitive, thin-skinned, maudlin. I mean to work hard, and show my uncle that I am worthy of the help he has given me. He has put me on the first rung of the ladder, and all he wants is to see me mount it like an honest man."

"Oh, Wilfred, I want something more than that," sighed Mrs. Dalrymple, too unintelligent in her worship of her son to understand his character, and to play a waiting game. "I want to see you Rosamund's husband."

"I'm sorry I can't oblige you to that extent; but if

you would open your eyes you would see that Rosamund and Ronald Halstead are in love with each other, and that there's nothing in this world to prevent their making a match of it."

"If you cared for your cousin you wouldn't stand by and let another young man snap her up. A young man without half your gifts."

"Perhaps I don't care for her in that way," answered Wilfred.

He was walking with his mother under the pollarded plane-trees, on the promenade by the lake, the rest of the party having mounted the Stanserhorn, intending to eat their luncheon on the summit, and come back to the "Lucernerhof" to tea. Wilfred had persuaded his mother to renounce an excursion that might be too fatiguing for her, and had kept her company in a drive by the lake, and a little modest shopping in the town. It was Sir William's practice to rest for a day or two at Lucerne on the homeward journey. He had his private sitting-room at the hotel, and spent his studious hours in luxurious solitude, while Rosamund made rapid excursions with Octavia and Ronald, unencumbered by any chaperon.

"It seems so extraordinary," murmured Mrs. Dalrymple in a complaining voice, "that you can live in that sweet girl's society day after day, and not adore her."

"Perhaps I have put a strong curb upon my feelings, mother. Perhaps I should adore her, if I saw any chance of being adored in return. But what is the use of my breaking my heart for a girl who doesn't care a straw for me?"

"But she would care for you—if you only took pains to please her—if you were properly attentive."

"Properly attentive. Would you have me push aside another man—fight for her travelling bag—snatch her wraps—like an officious footman? I tell you, mother, I've never been in the running. Pray don't let us argue the matter, or we shall quarrel. All you have to do is to take life easily, and all I have to do is to get on at the Bar. Consider the lilies, mother, and be sure that your brother will make things comfortable for you and Octavia in the future. Once having taken you under his wing he'll consider it his duty to provide for you."

"William is a dear, kind soul," assented Mrs. Dalrymple, dolefully, "but I have so built upon you and Rosamund falling in love with each other."

"'He builds too low who builds below the stars,'" quoted Wilfred, "there is no sandier foundation than a woman's heart."

"And I know that Octavia admires Ronald."

"You were counting on a double event! Every good woman is a matchmaker. When she has done with love and courtship in her own person her thoughts turn instinctively to the love affairs of the next generation—and she is inevitably wrong. Tell Octavia not to admire any man till he has begun to admire her."

"Rosamund never gives her a chance," grumbled his mother. "She appropriates Ronald in such a manner that it is impossible for him to pay the slightest attention to anyone else."

"And Ronald likes to be appropriated. He is a free spirit, a son of the wilderness. Be sure he would break away if the yoke galled him. There goes the third quarter after four. They'll be waiting tea for us if we don't hurry back."

Term had not begun when Sir William and his family settled down at Tangley Manor, and Wilfred spent most of his leisure in the family circle, where he was always welcomed by the most hospitable and kindest of uncles. He was really a worker, and was glad to get back to his orderly chambers, his law books, and the half-dozen modest briefs that were waiting for him on his table—ostentatiously displayed by the highly respectable clerk, whose services he shared with another stuff-gown on the same floor. He was by no means an unselfish young man, but he was honestly grateful to Sir William for the improvement of his position, and he was honest in his renunciation of Rosamund to a luckier lover.

"If I'd had the first innings I might have won," he told himself, "but Ronald is just the kind of fellow to please a girl who has known him all her life. His ugly mug would stand against him with a stranger. It wouldn't be love at first sight in his case."

Wilfred accepted the inevitable, and made himself agreeable to his cousin and her lover—looked on with resignation at a courtship which grew daily more marked. Ronald had given up—or at least indefinitely deferred—his Australian tour, and spent most of his life at Tangley, or upon various golf links and race-courses in the neighbourhood, always in Rosamund's company. Octavia was generally with them, but she was not the kind of young woman to be ignored by her companions, even when they were lovers, and she took her full share of the conversation and exacted considerable attention from Ronald.

She liked him better than any man she had ever met, and she may have thought that so long as the final words remained unspoken there was always a chance that his wandering fancies might turn from Rosamund to her. Seeing him intent upon out-door sports, more concerned in the result of an Australian cricket match than in a general election, or a discovery in science, she took him for one of those light-minded young men in whom constancy is not to be expected. She devoted herself to golf and lawn tennis as if her fate had depended on her success, and soon passed her cousin in both accomplishments.

She was convinced that the final words had not been spoken, and that Ronald was still free. Nor in their confidential talk had Rosamund ever confessed to any warmer feeling than friendship for her old play-fellow. She talked of him in her lightest tone, and made mock of his enthusiasm; but her face lit up at his coming, and she took no pains to conceal her pleasure in his society.

"Oh, we have always got on very well together," she would say. "Ronald is so good tempered, and thinks so little of himself. He is the most unselfish person—after my father—that I ever met with."

The pretty blush, the tender smile that emphasised this unsentimental appreciation would have told anyone how much she valued the man of whom she spoke so carelessly. Octavia understood her, but never invited her confidence. She was a very far-seeing young woman, and in the event of Ronald's inconstancy, she would have been able to declare that she had never supposed her cousin cared for him, except as an old play-fellow.

And so the time went on, and Mrs. Dalrymple's castles in the air had both collapsed. Ronald, who would have been such a splendid match for Octavia, showed no sign of wavering; and Rosamund preferred a commonplace young athlete, with rugged features, to the handsome and cultured Wilfred.

Mrs. Dalrymple thought of her daughter's ill-luck with resignation. Octavia was at least fortunate in having exchanged shabby lodgings for a luxurious home, and no doubt would be amply provided for by her uncle, if she remained a spinster. But the mother's affection for the gifted being whom Providence had permitted her to call her son was of a different quality. She keenly resented Rosamund's preference of the inferior man. She was one of those weak and impulsive women to whom it is given to love much and always to love unwisely. She would not acknowledge that Wilfred had no chance, and wearied him with her importunity—assuring him time after time that it would be his own fault if he did not win the prize.

"I have too much self-respect not to know when I am beaten, mother," he said, and, whether it was self-respect or mental indolence that influenced him, he abandoned hope, and stood out of the race, only coming to Tangley when it suited his convenience, generally on those pleasant Sundays when there were other visitors, his uncle's friends and chums of the Athenæum or the Garrick, men of the world, lawyers, doctors, journalists, authors, actors. Sir William had always been popular among such men, and although his happiest hours were spent in his library he had never withdrawn himself from the atmosphere of active life, and the newest developments of his century. He went often to his clubs, going to and fro modestly by rail, while he left the resources of the stable for his womenkind. He seldom dined away from home, preferring Rosa's company and the smiling hearth and admirable reading lamp to the finest assembly in Mayfair.

Winter came and passed. Ronald spent December on snowshoes in Canada, but stayed a shorter time than he had intended.

"I thought you were to be away two months," Rosa said when she welcomed his unannounced arrival, trying her hardest not to look too pleased.

"So did I; but—well, you see, there was something wanting in Canada."

"Had you bad weather?"

"The weather was perfection—but when it was best it set me thinking of Tangley—wondering whether the pond was frozen and you were skating on it—picturing you in your sealskins and sables, and wishing you were sleighing with me across a world of dazzling whiteness with a sapphire sky and a blinding sun. And then I remembered the Atlantic between us. One ought never to look for one's pleasures three thousand miles from one's friends."

"But you had friends at Montreal."

"Oh, yes, of a sort—jolly good fellows, pretty girls, everything that the heart of man could desire, except——"

The door opened, and Octavia came in before he could finish his sentence. She made no secret of her pleasure in seeing him. Her eyes sparkled and her cheeks flushed. She looked her handsomest. She really liked this strong, frank, outspoken young man, better than any man she had ever met, and she could not forget that he was rich, and that marriage with him would mean a prosperous life.

"I heard your voice in the hall," she said, "and could hardly believe my ears."

"Ain't it like a bore to turn up a month before I was expected? You are very good to be so cheery about it; but I daresay Sir William will think me a hopeless invertebrate sort of creature that never knows its own mind."

"He will think nothing of the kind. He will be delighted to have you among us again."

And then he had to be taken round the garden, to be shown all the old spots where they were so happy in the summer, albeit now there was only the barren neatly swept winter aspect, grass verdant, shrubs dark and glossy, the winter aconite shining like gold in sheltered borders under laurel hedges, but the cold December greyness over everything. It was the cosy afternoon hour before tea, the faint dusk creeping over the earth like a veil, lights beginning to shine in solitary windows here and there, above and below in the long front of the Georgian house, and in the drawing-room the vivid glow of a blazing fire, and the gay brightness of rose-coloured lamp shades. Everything suggested the peaceful fireside season, the time of drawn curtains and lamplight, books and homely music, long evenings that never seem too long where love is.

Ronald told his adventures by the drawing-room fire, at afternoon tea. He had only landed that morning, had spent an hour with his father, and had come straight to Tangley.

"I've left a portmanteau at the station," he said,

"so that if Sir William should ask me to stay I can snap at the chance. Cheek and forethought combined, eh?"

"Of course he will ask you," said Rosa, which charmed him.

"My brother never fails in hospitality," said Mrs. Dalrymple, which he thought officious and formal.

Hospitality forsooth! He didn't want the exercise of a virtue, but the welcome of a friend.

Sir William settled the question off-hand when he came in at seven o'clock by exclaiming, "My dear Ronald, this is very good of you. I saw your father at the club, and he told me you were coming to us. You have come to stay, of course?"

"If you really want me."

"Really and really. We've missed you every day of our lives. Get him a telegraph form, Rosa, and let him wire for his luggage."

"I don't think we need trouble about that, father."

And then Ronald confessed to the portmanteau at the station, and everybody laughed, while Sir William rang the bell and ordered a messenger to be sent for Mr. Halstead's luggage.

"There's a hat box, too," said Ronald, "for I know Rosa is very particular about church."

Sir William had left off thinking that to favour Ronald's suit was unfair to Wilfred. He had seen for some time past that his nephew had no chance. And Ronald's father was his oldest friend, and the man he would have chosen for Rosamund's father-in-law, and now he only waited for those two young hearts to find speech, and for the business to be despatched.

"They shall live with me," he told himself, "and make my grey hairs go down in cheerfulness to the grave. What would be the use of this roomy house and gardens to me without Rosa? It was bought for her sake, furnished to please her, and not a flower or a shrub has been planted with any other motive. They shall live with me. A fine, frank, noisy young man in my house will help to keep me alive."

Ronald stayed for a week, and on his praising the room Mrs. Dalrymple had given him—the tent room, so called after a striped paper which simulated the inside of a tent—Sir William said that it should be Ronald's room, and always ready for him.

"And you needn't leave your portmanteau at the station next time," said Sir William; "for you must consider yourself a son of the house—just as Wilfred is," he added, seeing that dark look on his sister's face, which he had seen there more than once when her son's interests seemed in jeopardy.

His forbearing temper excused that look. It was in human nature that a mother should be jealous for her idolised son. After all it was not a selfish feeling.

Sir William was all the kinder to Wilfred now that he knew there was no hope for him with Rosa. He slipped more than one handsome cheque into his nephew's hand between Michaelmas and Lady Day.

"I hope you make a good appearance at your chambers, Wilfred," he said. "Externals go for a good deal in your profession."

"Thanks to you, my dear uncle, my chambers are above the average—the lap of luxury as compared with the den I was in a year ago. Mother is to bring Rosa to tea the next time they are shopping in town, and if you would look in at the same time and see for yourself how much you have done for me——"

"No, no, my dear boy, I'll take Rosa's report. At my age a man is a creature of habit, and I hardly relish a cup of tea out of a certain quiet corner in the card room at my club—a cup of tea and a rubber of whist after it. I am old-fashioned enough to love that nearly extinct game."

"If you were once to try bridge——"

"I should never want to play whist again. That's what they all tell me, and that's why I'm determined not to try it—so long as I can make up a table. It is getting more and more of a favour."

The winter went gaily by, with modest dances at Hampton and in the neighbourhood, a good deal of cosy visiting in the Palace, and much of that simple gaiety which was all that Sir William desired for his daughter. Of metropolitan gaieties she knew nothing save the opera and the theatres. He had a wide circle of London friends, smart people among them, and could have launched his girl in London society had he so chosen. But he wanted to keep her to himself, in all her girlish simplicity, and he did not even recoil from those dreadful words, "middle-class" and "suburban," when he supervised the list of her local gaieties. If there was the taint of commerce, Stock Exchange, merchandise, in that pleasant neighbourhood of Hampton Court, the professional element was in the majority, and the barracks gave a pleasant military flavour to society. It was not all differences and exchanges, exports and imports.

Winter was gone, and it was early spring, the season of daffodils and afternoon tea by firelight. The winter dances were over, the fortunes of the football year were decided, and golf was more and more delightful, on the clear, dry afternoons, when the north-easter tweaked the noses of the players, and last year's leaves went whirling across the green.

Ronald had been coming and going all through the opening year, but it seemed that he came oftener than he went, for at every departure there was a promise of a speedy return. There was always a reason for his hurrying back. A football match, a race meeting, skating on the Hampton Court Water, golf, court tennis at the Palace, at which the cousins loved to look on, though Rosa had not yet mastered the mysteries of scoring for the royal game—and then someone in the Palace asked them to tea, and they walked home in the wintry dusk.

It was in one of those homeward walks that the prayer which had been in Ronald's heart for the last six months found its way to his lips.

It was early in March, and the daffodils were still shy of exposing their pale beauty to the nipping air. Ronald had been playing tennis with one of the soldiers from the barracks, and he and Mrs. Dalrymple and the two girls had been taking tea with an Indian General's widow in one of the pretty panelled drawing-rooms in King William's palace, and it was nearly dark when they set out on the homeward walk.

Perhaps it was a breach of manners on Ronald's part to leave mother and daughter to walk together in advance, while he hung behind with Rosa; but there are moments in life when a man's mind can hold only one thought, and for Ronald this was such a moment.

He was glad of the friendly dusk which hid his face, and gladder for the two mile walk between the Palace and Tangley.

Even with these advantages he was slow to find

speech, and when words did come they were woefully commonplace.

"Rosa, do you think a plain-headed fellow can ever be justified in asking a beautiful girl to take him for a husband?"

"What a queer question! Are you going to write an essay for the *World?*—'Plain and Pretty,' or something of that sort?"

"You know I'm not. Do answer a straight question."

"But it's such a difficult question!" said Rosa, trying to be flippant, but with a little shakiness in her articulation. "There's no knowing what you mean by plain-headed. I know when people say that of a horse one doesn't buy him. All his virtues go for nothing. Do you mean a monster?"

"No, or I might have said with two heads. No, Rosa, you know perfectly well what I mean. An honest, sunburnt, weatherbeaten chap, with all his features in the right place, but nothing to boast of in the way of form or outline—a rough-hewn chap that the most romantic girl in England couldn't exalt into a hero. Do you think such a man is an arrant coxcomb if he presumes to hope that the loveliest girl he ever saw will take him for what he's worth, just because he loves her to distraction?"

"You must be going to write an essay," faltered Rosa, "for you seem so dreadfully in earnest."

"Dreadfully, desperately, mortally in earnest; for all the happiness of my life hangs on your answer."

"Then why do you make it an abstract question?" said Rosa, this time with no attempt at flippancy. "If you are talking of your very own self—as the children say—*imprimis,* nobody at Tangley ever thought you plain."

"Never mind the rest. Can you put up with my looks if you are assured my heart and mind exist only to adore you?"

"Oh, Ronald, I don't ask for so much as that. I only want to be sure you love me," drawing a little nearer to him on the dark, lonely road, where the ripple of the invisible river made a musical accompaniment to their low voices, "nearly as much as I love you."

"Oh, Rosa, my angel, you lift me to the seventh heaven of mortal bliss!" he cried, in an ecstasy, encircling her with his strong arms, gathering her to his breast, raining kisses on her blushing face, heedless of the veil that covered it, and of the picture hat that he was annihilating.

"Ronald, don't behave like a cheap-tripper," she cried, extricating herself. "You make love like a Zulu, out of doors, where everybody can see you."

"I swear there's not a mortal in sight."

"If I were an East Ender I should be very angry with you about this hat," said Rosa, adjusting her disarranged finery. "Do you know it is my favourite? I thought it an inspiration the first day I wore it."

"Could one kiss spoil a hat?"

"Your great rough arm could."

"When you are my wife you shall have a new hat every day."

"Shall I? Then I presume you count upon an income of half a million a year."

"Are women's hats so dear?"

"Any price you like from ten pounds to five-and-sixpence; but I don't wear the five-and-sixpenny ones."

"Well, you shall have real diamonds in your hat instead of that paste thing that hurt my nose."

"The paste thing is the finest Brazilian. Father gave it me on my last birthday."

"That's why it nearly cut off my nose. Well, there seems nothing left for me to give you except my heart, and you have had that since you were eight years old —my airy, fairy Rosa, with short white skirts, long legs, and flying hair."

They talked all sorts of nonsense, in sheer gaiety of heart, for the rest of the way, and Octavia, tramping in silence by her mother's side—these two having really nothing left to say to each other—heard the gay voices and the laughter, and thought there could be no love making where there was so much gaiety. But in the corridor upstairs as they were going to their rooms to dress Rosa took her cousin's hand, squeezed it very hard, and whispered in her ear:

"Octavia, dearest, Ronald and I are engaged."

"Only just now," said Octavia mockingly. "You ought to have been ages ago, for you have always behaved like engaged lovers."

"Have we? Have I? Oh, Octavia, do you think I have been what Wilfred calls previous?"

"Stuff, child, I think you are very fond of him,

and you've been too candid to make believe you weren't."

It was a stab of a sort, and Octavia could not help giving it.

She went to her room and flung herself into her easy chair, and sat with her elbows on the arms of the chair, and her fists clenched, angry and tearless.

"The first brave, good man I ever knew," she said, "and he treats me like the dirt under his feet."

CHAPTER IV.

SIR WILLIAM RAYSON received the news of Rosa's engagement with cordial approval.

"Your father and I climbed the hill together, Ronald, and it is pleasant to me that we should be bound by new links on this calm table-land of our declining years."

"Not a word about declining, Sir William. You and my father are about the youngest men I know!"

"The world has used us kindly, my lad. We have worked hard, but we have loved our work, and love sweetens toil. Law has been his mistress, science mine, and we have been faithful. Sit down, and let us talk matters out."

They were in the library five minutes after the lovers had returned to the house, so eager was Ronald to make his happiness secure.

"I have seen this coming since those summer days at Tremezzo," said Sir William, leaning back in his capacious armchair, with the serene aspect of a man who has fought and won life's battle, and can take his rest after labour done. "I confess to you, Ronald, that till you appeared at the Villa I had been hoping that my nephew and Rosa might take a fancy to each other, so that in making them happy I might do the best possible thing for my sister, and only near relative."

"I don't think Dalrymple would have been the right man, sir, even had there been no such person as I—not another man in the world."

"That's uncomplimentary."

"Oh, I can see Dalrymple's merits, Sir William. He has talent, good looks, plenty of pluck, I daresay, but he's a hard-shelled sort of chap that would put his wife in the second place if she were the loveliest woman in England."

"You are not over generous to a vanquished rival. Well, perhaps Wilfred is a trifle hard—too keen upon cutting his own way through the world to have much heart left for other people. And I want Rosa to have the best that life can give—a devoted husband who will care more for her happiness than for his own!"

"I think I can promise as much as that, sir. It is very little to give for so dear a girl!"

"And can you be content to share my home, Ronald, and to let my last years be spent under the roof that shelters the child I love? It would be a hard thing for me to part with my girl, and I think you could both be happy in this house, and would not find me a domestic tyrant, or an exacting companion."

"My dear Sir William, there is no house in which I have been so happy—not even my father and mother's, though that is liberty hall—no house in which I could ever be happier."

"That's settled then. The house and all its appurtenances will be Rosa's, when I am gone. She will inherit everything I leave, for I intend to provide for my sister and her belongings before Rosa's marriage."

Ronald rushed up to Hyde Park Gardens next morning in time to surprise the judge at breakfast, and to impart his good news, and drove back to Tangley in the afternoon, escorting his mother, who was amiable but unwieldy, and took some time to get under way, her only idea of exercise being an hour's crawl in Kensington Gardens, with the three dogs whom she adored, and whose existence kept her in a state of perpetual anxiety, even in the peaceable seclusion of the gardens. She was an ideal wife and mother, never interfering with the liberty of husband or son, and believing in both as the most perfect of their species.

Ronald had to bear her company in her morning saunter, and to sympathise with all her anxieties about the three dogs, whether Toddie had canker, or Tags was footsore, or Tommy was not quite as lively as he ought to be; but though he succeeded in getting her back to Hyde Park Gardens before half-past one there was no moving her till nearly three, when, after keeping the carriage waiting a quarter of an hour while she changed her gown, they started for the long drive to Tangley.

"Why did you change your gown, mother? All your gowns are good."

"My dear, I was wearing a last year's gown. I should have been ashamed for those Dalrymples to have seen me in last year's sleeves. Mother and daughter are all eyes."

"And you are always good to look at, a handsome woman handsomely dressed."

"I was once, Ronnie, before I began to get fat. You know my photograph in your father's room."

"Yes, mother, and a charming portrait it is," said Ronald cheerfully, though it had always cost him a mental effort to realise that the slim-waisted, swan-necked young woman in a flounced skirt and long ear-rings was identical with the expansive matron he knew and loved.

They were at Tangley in time for tea, at which cosy meal the family were all assembled, Sir William having taken holiday from town and whist in honour of Rosa's engagement. Lady Halstead was overflowing with affection for her future daughter-in-law. She declared that she had been wishing for the engagement for ages, and had wondered at her Ronnie's slowness.

She looked the picture of happiness as she sat by the drawing-room fire with her sable mantle flung open to the advantage of a Parisian gown in dark-green cloth and rich velvet. She had the remains of a great beauty, a complexion of dazzling fairness, delicate features, and large blue eyes, fringed with gold, and in all her looks and ways an almost child-like candour and simplicity. Her only defect was that there was too much of her, an exuberant growth which seemed the result of sweet temper and prosperity.

Mrs. Dalrymple, thin, angular, wrinkled in advance of her years, observed her with a gloomy wonder.

"A woman who has always been rich," she thought, "who has never lived in dread of the rate collector, never turned her gown or had her boots mended, has never felt the iron wheel of poverty grinding her into the dust. Such a woman can hold her head high in spite of her sixteen stone."

That was Mrs. Dalrymple's difficulty. She could not feel quite at her ease among these prosperous people. She was not yet acclimatised to comfort and luxury, and could not forget the narrow lines on which her life had been running before her brother brought her to Tangley. All her attempts at supervising his household had run foul of this rock. She had been too anxious to curtail expenditure, and to prevent waste, and things were beginning to go wrong under her management, servants discontented, inferior tradesmen employed in the search of cheapness, when Octavia persuaded her to desist from troubling herself about a few pounds more or less, saved or wasted, and reminded her that her post at Tangley was that of chaperon and not housekeeper.

"If my uncle likes an extravagant cook, what does it matter to you and me?" she asked. "We shall be no poorer!"

Mrs. Dalrymple, who adored both her children, recognised the shrewdness of this counsel, and folded her housekeeping hands. She tried to feel at home in her luxurious surroundings, to wear her best gown without a harassing consciousness that she ought not to be wearing it; but contemplating Lady Halstead in her sables and French bonnet, the strings pinned with gems that flashed in the firelight, noting the placid smile, white hands, and soft piping voice, the woman who had been pinched and poor for the greater part of her life felt how much she had lost of this world's bliss; how little better her fate had been than that of the woman in the street, carrying a basket with the poor scraps for her husband's supper, bought from a costermonger's barrow.

Lady Halstead was overflowing with friendliness. Sir Henry was delighted, she assured them. The match had long been the desire of his heart. They must all come and dine in Hyde Park Gardens, "all of you," she repeated, looking at Octavia; it was quite the right thing that they should all dine together to mark the general satisfaction.

"Now, Sir William, when can you come?" she asked, turning to her old friend, who remembered her a sylph, a sylph with a handsome dowry, which had been one of Henry Halstead's stepping-stones towards the bench. "When have you all a free evening? We don't want a long notice, and we won't ask many people, just a cosy little party of ten or twelve."

"Is a dinner necessary?" asked Sir William, laughingly. "Cannot the sacrifice be avoided, seeing that we are all of one mind about the matter? Is it necessary to slay oxen and pour libations on the altar of an old friendship? I think not, Lady Halstead. Summer is coming. You and Harry can dine with us once a week if you like. You know our Sunday dinners."

"Indeed we do; and they are always charming."

"So you see where two families are so united, no pious orgies in the way of a family dinner can be needed."

"My dear little mother is a thoroughgoing Philistine," said Ronald, smiling down at her.

He had all sorts of jocosities about her bulk which seemed to take the sting out of it as a subject that need not be avoided.

The stately dinner-party was postponed indefinitely, and the year ran summerward along a path of flowers.

The Halsteads came to Tangley as often as Sir Henry's official duties and his wife's innumerable engagements would allow. Lady Halstead loved society, and went to a party of some kind nearly every night in the London season, and her diamonds, fair hair, and expanse of dazzling shoulders were a familiar appearance in many of the best houses. She was always pleasant, knew her world thoroughly and although there was so much of her she never seemed in the way.

The year ran summerward, and for Rosa and hèr lover it was a season of bliss without a shadow. In all their sports, their occupations, their thoughts, hopes, and ambitions, they were as one. Their future lay smooth and fair before them; and they loved to talk of that calm domestic life in which the dear father was to be the paramount figure.

"I never could have left my father," Rosa told her lover. "No, sir, though I love you to distraction—as I've been foolish enough to let you see—had it come to a choice between you and him, you would have been nowhere."

"And I love you all the better for your faithfulness to that good man. But what should I have done if my people had wanted me to live with them?" asked Ronald, with a serio-comic ruefulness. "They might, you know; there's plenty of room in Hyde Park Gardens and in the place up the river."

"It would have been embarrassing, but we could have gone to them sometimes—for a week."

"We shall have to do that as it is, and we'll make it Henley week. Luckily my mother is too much of a Philistine to suggest a joint household. She'd think it un-English, and that your maid and hers would quarrel. My mother is British to the core. And she highly approves of our living with Sir William—for otherwise, she says, he would be very likely to marry again."

"Marry again? My father!"

"Such things have been done. Sir William is not much over sixty."

"There is not a woman in the world good enough for him. No, Ronnie, no daughter of Heth shall come and steal him from us. He is going to be happy with us all the days of our life."

She would not say his life. She would not let herself remember that their lives were not on the same plane. She could not imagine her existence without that loving father who had been all the world to her from her dawn of reason.

Time wore on. There were Sunday parties and week-day parties at Tangley, open house always for pleasant neighbours and old friends from London; and among the old friends came Reginald Honeybill, who had never been a friend of the famous physician, but who had contrived to edge himself into the circle on the strength of a casual acquaintance of thirty years.

Mr. Honeybill had suffered from the ravages of time in character and social status, and had degenerated from the man about town to the drawing-room gossip, attaching himself mostly to the feminine side of the houses he visited. He had turned vegetarian and tee-totaler, and talked learnedly upon medical matters, knew the names and qualifications of Continental doctors, and was a great authority upon "cures," always ready to diagnose a case, and to name the exact spring that would bring healing.

"Not the sulphur!" he would exclaim to a friendly dowager. "My dear lady, with the symptoms you describe sulphur is rank poison. The saline—nothing but the saline! Three glasses before breakfast, and three little walks between the glasses; a milk pudding for lunch, and two more glasses in the afternoon, with a long walk after each," and so on, and so on. Medicine had become Reggie's hobby. He almost fancied himself a doctor; but he was very careful not to air his medical knowledge before Sir William Rayson.

Here, as elsewhere, he attached himself to the ladies of the family. Rosa remembered her father's contempt, and avoided him as much as she could. Octavia thought him good-natured and amusing. Mrs. Dalrymple liked him best of all her brother's visitors, and defended him stoutly against masculine sneers. He paid her more attention than any other friend of the house, though all who came were courteous to Sir William's sister, even when not quite liking the woman. Reginald Honeybill would sit in her pocket, and tell her things about smart people. To know him was a fashionable education. From him she caught the tricks of speech and ways of thinking of that other world from which poverty had excluded her. She was never tired of that vacuous gossip which her beloved Wilfred had held in contempt, and had never brought home—the West End scandals, true or false, the glimpses behind the scenes, the open secrets. Reggie's scandals and his medical theories alike charmed her. Perhaps the former were no more veracious than the latter, but they served Reggie's turn with Mrs. Dalrymple and a good many other people. An intelligent little man who liked to sit by the fire and drink tea, and who knew all about everybody's inside, was welcome in a good many drawing-rooms and boudoirs. He always had the last word about an illustrious invalid, Cabinet Minister, or great lady, would prophesy cure or death, could describe the course of the malady, and knew what the doctors had said in consultation.

"As if he had been listening at the door," a malevolent man-creature said of him.

When the June roses were blooming in the Tangley gardens, this friendship had advanced so far that Mrs. Dalrymple had taken to telling Reggie her troubles much more freely than she told them to Octavia or Wilfred, since her daughter generally disagreed with her, and her son sometimes snubbed her. Among the scattered groups in the garden on a Sunday, after lunch or after tea, Mr. Honeybill and Mrs. Dalrymple were often to be seen seated side by side in basket chairs, or sheltered cosily in a tent made for two.

"I have never understood Honeybill's place in creation," Sir William said to Sir Henry, "but now I find there is a use for him. He amuses my sister."

On one particular Sunday afternoon — when the young people were playing croquet with a seriousness worthy of a cabinet council during a crisis—Mrs. Dalrymple was more than usually confidential, and more than usually egotistical, and it argued some amiability upon Reggie's part that he could listen with bland patience, while she lamented her hard case.

"Rosamund's wedding day was settled last night," she said. "It is to be the 20th of September, and they are to spend their honeymoon at Tremezzo, so you see there will be no Italy for my children and me this year."

"But could not you join them at the villa a month or so later, when they are old married people?"

"I have not been asked, Mr. Honeybill. There has not been the slightest allusion to our autumn holiday. Indeed, I know no more what my fate and my poor daughter's is to be—after Rosamund's wedding—than I know who is to be the next President of the French Republic."

"No doubt Sir William will consider your comfort."

"He ought to do so, Mr. Honeybill. He ought to remember that I broke up my home, and separated myself from my only son, in order to be useful to him."

"And you have had a very good time ever since, and you ought to be grateful," thought Honeybill, and had he known that the "home" consisted of four shabbily furnished rooms in a shabby street, and that the breaking-up process consisted of giving the landlady a week's notice and packing three or four trunks, he would have thought so all the more.

"It is a hard thing to be taken up by a near relative and dropped again, Mr. Honeybill."

"Oh, but I can't believe Sir William means to drop you. Your brother is a thoroughly good sort. If I had a near relation like him, I should take no more heed of ways and means than the lilies of the field. You are all right."

"I suppose you know that Octavia and I are to leave Tangley?"

"Well, I should have guessed as much. The house would hardly be large enough for you and Miss Dalrymple and Sir William and the young couple. It would make it too much like a hydro."

"Perhaps you do not know that there are five

spare bedrooms," said Mrs. Dalrymple severely. "But I am the last person in the world to wish to stay where I am not wanted, though I must say I think my brother's plan of having Rosa and her husband to live with him, instead of giving them a nice little house in the neighbourhood, and remaining sole master of his own, will shorten his life."

"You think there may be bothers and misunderstandings?"

"How can that be avoided? My brother likes repose, a studious retirement; and how will he relish Mr. Halstead's men friends—noisy creatures, always talking of cricket or rowing—pouring into the house at all hours in their flannels, and wanting all sorts of irregular meals?"

"That's a dark picture! But I think Halstead will have some discretion; and Sir William adores his daughter, and will object to nothing so long as she is happy."

"Perhaps not, poor dear! But the whole thing makes me think of King Lear."

"Oh, not quite so bad as that. Sir William will keep the sinews of war, and will be master of the situation."

"He is parting with half his fortune, I suspect, for his daughter's marriage settlement."

"Lucky girl! there are not many such fathers nowadays. There is something positively romantic in such affection. By the way, I think you told me you never met your brother's wife?" pursued Honeybill, looking at her sharply, with his hawk-bill nose on one side, and his eyes screwed up as if he were taking aim at something.

"Met her, Mr. Honeybill! Why, I have never so much as heard her maiden name."

"And you never will hear it."

"But why should it be kept from me?"

"Because—because—Mrs. Dalrymple, are you a woman one can trust? If I tell you my real opinion about your brother's marriage—will you keep it to yourself, and never breathe a syllable of what I am going to say?"

"I can be as secret as the grave," she said eagerly.

"And you will?"

"On my word of honour."

"Well, then, between friends, and with all respect

for a good man who has done more than one man in a thousand would do to atone for a youthful error, I believe your brother's marriage is a myth. He was far too distinguished a man twenty years ago—when his professional career was at the zenith—to be able to conceal his marriage from every mortal who ever knew him. I have talked to any number of his friends, and not one of them ever saw his wife or heard anything about his marriage. He was always there—to the front—in Cavendish Place, dining out and giving dinners all the year round, and his house was open to all his friends. Where was the wife in those days?"

"In a villa twenty miles away, perhaps."

"Villas are always discovered and talked about. My dear lady, that wife is a myth."

"But there is Rosamund."

"A daughter, yes—we admit the daughter."

"And you think that she is—that she is—not his heiress?" Mrs. Dalrymple exclaimed breathlessly.

A wide horizon opened as she spoke. She and her children were Sir William's natural heirs, she told herself, were he to die without legal issue.

"No, my dear Mrs. Dalrymple, I think nothing of the kind. You may be sure—whatever the circumstances of the young lady's birth may be, Sir William has made a will that nobody can impugn, and that she will inherit the bulk of his fortune."

"To the injury of his nephew and niece. If—if you are right, Mr. Honeybill, my brother will be guilty of a great injustice!"

"Come, come, dear lady, that is going a little too far," murmured Reggie soothingly. "Every man has a right to follow the bent of his own natural affections —and even if there is a bend sinister—well, Miss Rayson is a daughter of whom any parent might be proud—and it can make very little difference."

"Nothing makes any difference nowadays," said Mrs. Dalrymple gloomily. "We live in an age in which all barriers are broken down."

"And a very pleasant age it is," chirruped Reggie. "Heaven forbid we should build the barriers up again."

"To my mind such a state of things is horrible!" said Mrs. Dalrymple. "Our parents were people of the highest principles—people who had no indulgence for wrong-doing—and how my brother William—reared in an evangelical home—could ever——"

"Perhaps that was the reason," murmured Reggie.

"But you must tell me your ground for forming this—this dreadful opinion."

"My dear lady, if I had known you would take it so seriously, I would never have mentioned my opinion. I had no such solemn views about Sir William's youthful frailties. However, let us gossip it out. I saw a good deal of your brother during a visit to Sir George Chilworth's shooting lodge in Argyllshire, some fifteen years ago. I venture to think he liked my society. Halstead was our fellow guest, then a rising Q.C., and a very entertaining companion, full of anecdote, mostly legal—those lawyers are beggars to talk shop. We were a very cheery party, till our social comedy ended suddenly by the tragical death of our host."

"Murdered by his wife! I have not forgotten the story."

"Well, during the three weeks that preceded the tragedy, I had ample opportunities of seeing your brother and Lady Chilworth together, and although he exercised the most perfect command over himself, and never once passed the limits of an old-established friendship, I saw that he adored her."

"Could he be so weak?"

"As to let me pluck out the heart of his mystery? Well, you see, dear Mrs. Dalrymple, I am a very keen observer, and it needs but a speck of thistledown to show me which way the wind is blowing, where another man would want a semaphore. I saw that William Rayson had loved that woman from the time they first met—at Naples—years before. She was not in her first youth—nearer thirty than twenty I should say. They used to talk of Italy—to talk of the old days at Sorrento, and she let him see that she was not happy. In short, it was a clear case—for a man with sympathies—and eyes and ears."

"She must have been a brazen-faced creature."

"She was not the modest violet, hiding among its leaves; but she was a splendid woman. I never saw her superior in beauty or in charm."

"But what was the cause of her madness—for, I suppose, she was mad when she shot her husband?"

"We have your brother's word for that."

"But you must have seen signs of derangement in

those three weeks you spent in the same house with her."

"No, I can recall nothing that suggested a mind distraught—though she had fitful spirits, and was always doing eccentric things—or, at least, eccentric enough to annoy that starched politician, her husband. On the afternoon of his death, she had tramped to the post-office through a blinding rain to send a telegram, and there is no doubt Sir George was furious, and that they quarrelled on the way home, and then in a fit of rage—or madness—she snatched up one of his pistols and sent a bullet through his heart. Perhaps it was the first proof she ever had that he possessed one."

"But I don't quite follow you—about Rosamund. What has this to do with her?"

"Only that she is the living image of Lady Chilworth."

"What?"

"There is not a feature in her face that is not formed upon the same model. In complexion—in figure—even in the tones of her voice now and then—the unfortunate lady I met in Argyllshire lives again."

"And you think——"

"I think that the only rational explanation of the mystery is that this woman was your brother's mistress before she was George Chilworth's wife."

"Is that possible? Could Sir George have tolerated William's presence in his house if that were so?"

"He may not have known the truth. Some secrets are well kept—or he may have known, and condoned the past. Such things have been."

"I cannot believe it," said Mrs. Dalrymple, with a pious air; and yet she did believe, and her mind was wandering in a labyrinth of wild conjectures. A child born out of wedlock—the nameless daughter of an Italian adventuress, the star of a *café chantant,* a creature with loose morality and cracked brain. This miserable waif was to inherit Sir William's fortune, was to marry Sir Henry Halstead's only son, and so join wealth to wealth, while her son and daughter, her brother's natural heirs, were to have nothing or only such paltry legacies as their uncle might leave them, for decency, and to avoid the risk of a disputed will! It seemed to her a case of intolerable injustice, an infamous wrong. She had thought it unjust even before she knew of this dark secret, even when Rosamund's claims were unimpeached

—but now it seemed an iniquity against which the strong arm of Providence ought to stretch itself.

"Mr. Honeybill," she said, with freezing dignity, "I must beg that you never again mention this subject in my hearing. My respect and affection for my brother forbid my listening to a single word that tends to lower him in my esteem."

"My dear lady, since you have heard—and I may say have elicited from me, all the words that I have to say upon this subject, there can be no occasion to recur to it. I had no idea you would make a tragedy of my little bit of conjectural gossip. After all, you know, it is only conjecture. Let's go and watch the croquet, and don't let us be solemn. It is much too warm and too pleasant here among the midsummer roses for anybody to treat anything seriously."

CHAPTER V.

FROM the hour of that Sunday afternoon conversation with Reginald Honeybill, Mrs. Dalrymple's thoughts dwelt almost unceasingly upon the mystery of Rosamund's existence. She was for ever on the alert for new lights, and noticed every word that fell from her brother's lips, in the hope of finding a clue to his secret. Yet of what advantage would it be to her to ferret out Rosamund's history, since nothing would alter the girl's position as Sir William's heiress? Such a disposal of his wealth might be an injustice that cried aloud to Heaven for vengeance, but William Rayson had made his own fortune, and would choose his own heir.

Mrs. Dalrymple prided herself upon being a good Churchwoman, went to church twice on Sundays, never missed a Saint's day, and attended matins all the week. She had been brought up in an atmosphere of evangelical piety, by parents from whose narrow views

William Rayson early broke away, and threw in his lot with the scientists, at a time when Darwin's name was a sound of horror to people of his parents' way of thinking. Even Margaret Rayson's narrower mind had wearied of the home teaching, and after her marriage, on finding herself a free agent, with a husband of no religion, she became an Anglican of the Anglicans, learned in forms and ceremonies, but with a mind that had never been illumined with one ray of light from the inner sanctuary of the Temple.

She was one of a large body of Englishwomen with whom early hours and church-going constitute the beginning and end of Christianity; and it had never occurred to her that her feelings with regard to her brother and her brother's child were to the last degree un-Christian. She was a shallow-brained woman, soured by the disappointments and difficulties of her married life, and with one absorbing passion, her love for her children.

She suspected that Octavia had something more than a friendly liking for Ronald Halstead, and she hated to see the lovers together in their exultant happiness, while her girl was left in the background, the object of no delicate attentions, no exclusive regard. Rosamund was full of affection and kindness for her cousin, and gave herself no triumphant airs in the possession of a devoted lover; but Rosamund's affection was not enough for Mrs. Dalrymple, who wanted her daughter to be first, not second, in the family circle. And then she had such an arduous part to play to sympathise with her brother's delight in his daughter's happiness, to be interested in every detail of Rosamund's expensive trousseau, in the improvements and re-arrangements that were to be made in the spacious old house for the young people's comfort, Rosa's new morning-room, which was to be next Ronald's smoking-room; the little blue bedroom which was to be Ronald's dressing-room; while, in confidential moments, when she and Sir William were alone she was expected to chime in with his ideas of future alterations on the upper floor when rooms should be wanted for nurseries.

Sir William loved to look forward to those patriarchal days, when the companion of his later life, the creature he loved best on earth, might be the mother of a joyous brood.

"And you needn't be afraid about your future," he said, after one of these discussions, patting his sister's hand affectionately. "Be sure things will be made comfortable for you."

Comfortable! The word inspired no confidence. Two or three hundred a year, perhaps, Mrs. Dalrymple thought, as a set-off against all the amenities of Tangley Manor.

And so the summer went by, a season of unclouded bliss for Rosamund and her lover, and the first shadow that fell across love's rosy path came when summer was at its ripest, and the sickle was in the corn. It came with the lovers' first parting in the second week of August, when Ronald went up to Scotland to shoot with Sir Henry, who for the last ten years had rented a small moor a dozen miles from Perth, and who counted upon having Ronald during some part of the long vacation, the only season when he had leisure to enjoy his son's society.

This year Ronald had wanted not to go. Leave Rosa? Not for all the grouse that ever flew!

"Not for the grouse, Ronnie, but to please your

father. Sir Henry would be dreadfully disappointed if you were not with him at Braeside."

"Did my father tell you that?"

"No, it was Maman."

Maman was the endearing name that Rosa had given Lady Halstead, who had begged to be called mother. Rosa shrank from giving that name to anyone, except to the unremembered mother, the dream-phantom which sometimes flitted across her slumbers.

"I cannot remember my mother," she faltered, "but I don't think I could call anyone by the name that was hers. Let me call you Maman, dear Lady Halstead. It sounds just as loving."

Sir Henry was not slow to express himself.

"I daresay Rosa thinks me a selfish old beggar for wanting Ronald at Braeside; but my holiday would be no holiday without him. You see, my shooting is the smallest thing in that line, and I have never asked any guns outside my family. I have always relied on Ronald for company, except when he was on the other side of the world," he said in one of the happy Sunday afternoons when the family were collected round the tea-table in the garden, with Rosamund and Octavia to pour out tea and give employment to Wilfred and Ronald and a couple of cavalry men from Hampton Court in waiting upon their elders: Lady Halstead in mauve foulard and a mauve chiffon hat, large and lovely, overflowing the biggest of the wicker chairs, and slowly waving a futile black lace fan; Mrs. Dalrymple neatly dressed in a gown of the kind that dressmakers call "material," a something that was neither silk nor wool, in colour a dull slate-grey, patterned with spade-aces in black and white—one of those hideous gowns which such women choose with an unerring preference for the ugly; Sir Henry in the lightest grey suit his tailor could be persuaded to make for him; and Sir William in a slightly darker greyness.

"Now, I know you think me selfish, my dear," repeated Sir Henry, who had brought his chair to the tea-table and seated himself at Rosamund's elbow. "But you must remember that you can come to Braeside with Ronald next August; and that if your father had been a little quicker about the wedding, you could have come with him this year. The house is very small, but we'd have found room for you two."

"It would have been too lovely," said Rosa gaily;

"and I count on being there next year. Perhaps Ronnie can teach me to load the guns, or do something useful. And I don't think you are a scrap selfish, Sir Henry, and I should be very angry with Ronald if he thought of disappointing you."

"But I do think of it," said Ronald in a bass growl. "The governor can get another gun if he likes. He has lots of pals whose company suits him as well as mine."

"Ronald, remember the fifth commandment," said Rosa, shaking a tea-spoon at him. "Your days will be very short in the land if you behave like this. He is going to Braeside, Sir Henry, in good time for the twelfth, and I am not going to be the least bit unhappy about it. Indeed, I shall be glad to get him out of the way; for I have been very casual about my trousseau up to now, and I shall want most of the time for the dressmakers."

"My dear Rosa, don't have too many gowns," said Lady Halstead, in a warning voice. "The worst dressed women are the women with too many gowns. Make them give you the newest thing from Paris, and wear it out in a month. Twelve walking gowns and six evening gowns a year are enough for any reasonable woman."

"And the tea gowns?" asked Sir Henry.

"Oh, for a child like Rosa a Liberty thing for nine or ten pounds will do, and that needn't count."

"I see that on your rational lines a woman might contrive to dress herself respectably for a thousand a year," said Sir William.

"I don't believe I spend as much as that, not on actual clothes," replied Lady Halstead, with a superb carelessness.

So, after much light talk, it was decided that Ronald was to shoot grouse with his father, and when all the Sunday company had gone and Sir William gave Rosa his good-night kiss, he added a word of praise for her unselfishness.

"But I'm afraid you'll miss your Ronnie sadly, all the same," he said.

"Not while I have you, father."

Yet in spite of her affection for her father, and the perfect sympathy between them, Rosamund did sorely miss the devoted lover, the strong, cheery voice, the light-hearted companion, who had made himself part of her life. Not for worlds would she have allowed her father to see any sign of low spirits or repining, but her eager delight in Ronald's daily letter was enough to show how dearly he was loved, and how much he must be missed.

The first ten days after the parting were spent in drives and walks with Sir William, who deserted his club, declaring that all his friends were away, and in shopping and dressmaking visits in London, with a concert and theatre thrown in. And these were days of tranquil pleasantness, despite that ever-present want of the other person whose society had become a matter of course.

Much as she might regret Ronald's absence, Rosa could not be unhappy while she had her father's company, together with those long rambling letters which came every morning and kept her informed of all that was doing at Braeside. Boxes of grouse had come also from Sir Henry's moor, but of those Rosamund kept no account.

So far the time of Ronald's absence had been a season of mitigated regret; but a telegram received at the family breakfast-table changed the happy atmosphere of Rosamund's home to dullness and despondency.

Sir William's grave countenance as he read the message filled her with sudden fear.

"Oh, father, is there anything wrong?" she cried. "Is it about Ronald—an accident?"

The possibility of gun accidents had seldom been absent from her thoughts since her lover's departure, and now her father's look of grave distress seemed to announce doom.

"No, no, my dear, Ronald is well enough," Sir William answered hastily, with his eyes still on the message.

"The telegram is not about him—really—really?" Rosa questioned with anxious looks.

"No, no—nothing to do with him. No answer," to the servant who stood waiting.

Mrs. Dalrymple was watching her brother's countenance almost as earnestly as Rosa. What could it mean? Something very serious, assuredly, for there was grave trouble in Sir William's face as he rose from the table and walked slowly out of the room.

Was he deceiving his daughter, Mrs. Dalrymple

wondered. Had some harm happened to Rosa's lover, which her father wanted to hide from her at first, to put off the evil hour in which he must tell her news that might break her heart? There had been something in his tone—a touch of carelessness in his answer to his daughter—that disposed Mrs. Dalrymple to think the telegram was no message of woe for Rosa. But it brought bad news for Sir William. Of that there could be no doubt. She took upon herself a sister's privilege and followed him to his library—where she found him standing with a railway guide in his hand, and his body-servant in attendance.

"One portmanteau will be enough—yes, and a hat-box," he said, and then, turning sharply on his sister as the man left the room, "What do you want, Margaret?"

"I am afraid you have had troublesome news, William."

"Nothing that can trouble this house. I am going to—to friends in the North."

"Don't say to Scotland, William. Oh, don't say you've been summoned to Scotland."

"Why not?"

"If anything has happened to Ronald, it will break Rosa's heart."

"Didn't you hear me say that nothing had happened? I am going away—for a week—or possibly longer, and I must ask you and Octavia to do all that affection can do to make Rosa happy. It is hard lines for me to leave her while Ronald is away—but I know how kind you will be. You must do all you can to interest her in her trousseau. Take her up to London every day if you like; and give her plenty of music. I know I can rely on you."

"It would be hard if you couldn't, William."

"Yes, yes, of course. You're her aunt—and if you weren't you couldn't help being fond of her. You have known her long enough to know what a lovable being she is," holding out his hand to his sister in frank affection. "There, there! I shall have only a few minutes to bid her good-bye while the dog-cart is coming round."

"Are you going by the ten-fifty?"

"Yes—send Rosa to me at once."

He took Rosamund into the garden, and pacing slowly up and down the lawn, he told her that business of an unexpected and troublesome nature was taking him to the North of England; but there was nothing in the trouble that concerned either Rosamund or himself, or anyone she knew. So all she had to do was to make herself as happy as she could during his absence, which would not last one hour longer than he could help.

Her lips trembled, her eyes filled with tears; but as she had tried to be brave when her lover left her, so she tried to be brave now. Only it was a worse parting, for the feeling of an unknown trouble spread round her like a cloud.

"You are not unhappy, father?" she asked anxiously.

"No, no, dear; never while all is well with you."

"And you are not going into any danger?"

"Danger? No. I am going to travel two or three hundred miles in as much comfort as modern improvements can give me; and if you were able to compare the style of travelling with my journeys of forty years ago you would know how little reason I have to complain. I hear the cart coming round. Good-bye, my dearest treasure, and God be with you till we meet again."

He took her in his arms and kissed her with unwonted fervour.

"My dear, dear child," he murmured, with a deep sigh.

They had been parted before to-day, but never for more than two or three days at a time, and at long intervals. Once or twice in a year Sir William had left home on a business journey, as he was leaving to-day, and his journey had always been to the North. But his face had never worn the troubled look it had to-day, nor had he ever left his daughter without specifying the time of his return.

She stood on the gravel drive while he took his seat in the cart, and held up her hand to him for a last good-bye; and it seemed to her as if all the gladness had gone out of her life when the dog-cart disappeared at a turn of the avenue. Wilfred, summoned by a maternal telegram, came to dinner that evening, and devoted himself to Rosamund, making her play and sing to him, hanging over the piano, trying to interest her in spite of herself in his talk of books, and plays, and the famous people with whom he rubbed shoulders in London, and of the last interesting trial suitable for home discussion. She was interested, to a certain degree, giving him half her mind, while the other half was travelling painfully on an unknown journey to "the North," with the father she adored. She had only once before to-day seen that look of grief and trouble in Sir William's face, and that was years ago, when, as a child, she questioned him about her mother.

Wilfred came next day, and the next after that, bringing a new Paderewski waltz, and a new novel, for his cousin.

"I am not going to leave you three lone lorn women without the protection of a black coat," he said, laughing; "but I hope you don't all think me a consummate bore for coming every night."

"Nobody can expect a mother to think her son a bore," Mrs. Dalrymple said somewhat sourly, after waiting for Rosamund to protest; "but perhaps Rosa considers every young man *de trop* except Ronald."

"Oh, aunt, how can you say such a thing? And

when Wilfred is so clever, and takes so much trouble to amuse us."

"Worse and worse, Rosamund," said Wilfred. "That is the exact description of a bore. He takes trouble to amuse—a painstaking dullard, whose laborious vivacity gets on everybody's nerves."

"You know I don't mean that. I think it very kind of you to try to fill my father's place while we are so lonely."

This went on for about ten days, Wilfred appearing every evening before dinner, and early on Saturday afternoon for a game at croquet, which he played well enough to make him worth beating, though he was greatly inferior to Ronald at this and all games, an inferiority that vexed him, as it marked the difference between the young man who had to earn his bread and the young man who hadn't.

He spent the whole of Sunday at Tangley, arriving in time for the morning service, so as to be able to discuss the Rector's ritualistic leanings, and the quality of the new organ.

It was a splendid August day, and the family spent the afternoon in the gardens, where there came visitors from London, and among others Mr. Honeybill, looking divinely cool in a pale grey *complet* and a white Homburg hat.

He had just come from Homburg, where he pronounced the season to have been exceptionally brilliant—seasons always were brilliant when he was among the mob—and where he appeared to have lived in the lap of royalty. And now he was passing through town on his way to Ayrshire, and could not resist the temptation to run down and see the dear ladies at Tangley.

"You all ought to have been at Homburg," he said, shaking his finger at Rosamund, "instead of moping in this garden all through August."

"I assure you there has been no moping, and we are much happier here than among a crowd of people we don't know," Rosa answered, with a little resolute air with which she meant to keep Mr. Honeybill in his place.

She knew that her father disliked him, and disliked him herself for that reason, and perhaps from an instinctive distrust of so artificial a creature.

"But you ought to know them, Miss Rayson," protested Honeybill, "and they ought to know you! It is too bad of Sir William to keep you like a nun in an enclosed convent, when you ought to be seeing your name and your frocks in all the society papers. 'What shall I wear to be for ever known?' That is what every young lady nowadays asks herself when she gets up in the morning. And here are you and Miss Dalrymple spending whole mornings in Sloane Street, and buying mountains of clothes, without so much as a line in a halfpenny paper."

"It is very middle-class of us, no doubt," said Rosa, "but then, you see, we don't mind being middle-class. We have no proper ambition."

Mr. Honeybill transferred his attentions to the lady who knew how to appreciate his versatile gifts. Alas! it had been borne in upon him of late that he was no longer esteemed at his proper value by youth and beauty. The up-to-date young woman—as he met her in London and in country houses—had got beyond him. The progress of society had been too rapid for even his keen intelligence. It was impossible at five-and-forty to keep well to the front in the movement of modern life. There was no halting-place, no rest for the sole of his foot, in the progress of folly. The young women had begun to call him good fun. They patronised him, and called him a sweet old thing, and said things before him, holding his presence of no account in the *Bona dea* assemblies. He was "only Reggie." For appreciation he now must look to the mothers and aunts; and among these he was sure of his ground. The cosiest of the bachelor bedrooms, the most luxurious armchair in the morning-room, were kept for Mr. Honeybill, when the mistress of the house was over forty.

This afternoon, Mrs. Dalrymple took him to look at the grape-houses, which were at the end of a long walk, where, sheltered from the north-east by an old red-brick wall, there was a broad herbaceous border, on which Rosamund had lavished thought and care. The gaudy autumn flowers made a blaze of colour on this sunny afternoon, and on the other side of the walk an iron paling divided the garden from the little park, where Rosamund's Jersey cows enjoyed the placid monotony of their lives, so idle, yet so useful.

"That old wall with the flowers in front of it is quite the prettiest bit of your garden," said Reggie, stopping by a rustic bench. "Do let us sit down and admire it."

"Don't call it my garden, Mr. Honeybill. I am to bid good-bye to Tangley in a few weeks," remonstrated Mrs. Dalrymple, as she seated herself.

She was one of those women who cannot keep their grievances to themselves.

"Oh, but you will be near your brother, and always dropping in upon the young people," answered Reggie, taking his place at her side, and admiring his shoes, which were made by the one man in London who could make shoes, as his clothes, hat, and gloves were made by the only possible makers of those articles.

"No, indeed, I shall not. Dearly as I love my brother William—the only near relation I have in the world except my children—I shall never enter these gates uninvited."

"Oh, well, the invitations will come thick and fast, no doubt. Your niece won't be able to get on without you and her cousin."

"Octavia can do as she likes, Mr. Honeybill, but I hope I have some self-respect."

"Of course!" said Reggie, who thought this woman

was the silliest he had ever met with, and he was a student of silly women.

"Is Sir William going to be long away?" he asked.

"He talked of a week, but he has been gone ten days, and there is no talk of his return."

"Has he gone to Scotland to shoot?"

"Oh, dear, no! He never cared much for sport of any kind, and he has done no shooting of late years. I fear it was nothing as pleasant as shooting that took him away at a moment's notice."

And then she told Honeybill the story of the telegram, Sir William's troubled manner, and sudden journey.

"To the North?" repeated Honeybill. "Did that mean Scotland?"

"He did not say Scotland."

"Strange!" mused Honeybill. "Strange that he should hurry off in that direction ten days ago!"

"Why strange?"

"Life is full of strange things, Mrs. Dalrymple," returned Honeybill, with his philosophical air. "You may remember our little gossip about Lady Chilworth a few weeks ago?"

Yes, Mrs. Dalrymple remembered, having, indeed, occupied her mind with little else than the train of thought Honeybill had started, in his airy way.

"Well, I have often thought of that poor lady, and her tragical story—during the years that have gone by since the murder—but I have thought of her a little more, perhaps, since our conversation; seeing you so keenly interested in the notion which I ventured to touch upon in strictest confidence, of course, as to a woman of the world, of whose perfect discretion I was assured."

"Yes, yes, I understand. But what then?"

The question was asked with breathless eagerness, the lady forgetting that she had forbidden Mr. Honeybill ever to recur to the subject in her hearing.

"Things fall out curiously. You say Sir William started for the North—probably Scotland—ten days ago, that is to say one day later than the event described in this paragraph which I cut out of a Glasgow paper."

He had opened his letter-case—a thing of lizard-skin and four-leaved shamrocks in beaten gold, gift of one of his middle-aged admirers—and extracted a slip of newspaper, which he handed to Mrs. Dalrymple, whose eager eyes devoured the following paragraph:—

"ESCAPE OF A CRIMINAL LUNATIC.

"Lady Chilworth, whom our readers may remember as being tried for the murder of her husband in a fit of insane fury, sixteen years ago, and who has been kept in confinement in the Government Asylum at Hatterick ever since, managed to effect her escape yesterday morning before daybreak, and has not yet been traced. It is suspected that she must have been helped by someone within the walls, as an attempt at evasion would seem hopeless to anyone acquainted with the rules of the institution and the plan of the building and its surroundings. Lady Chilworth's health had deteriorated for some time past, and her outbreaks of insanity had increased in violence. It is feared that she may attempt to destroy herself, unless speedily found."

"The newspaper containing that paragraph was sent me by a sporting friend who wanted me to see the notice of his big shoot, and it was only by chance that I happened to come upon that bit of news—since in such cases one generally reads the marked paragraph, and throws the paper away. Curious, ain't it, Mrs. D.?"

"Then this mad woman is roaming about the country?" said Mrs. Dalrymple.

"Unless she has drowned herself in the nearest river, which seems likely!"

"And you think my brother went——"

"To help in the search for her? Yes; remembering what I do remember of his interest in that unhappy woman, I should think he would want to see the last of her."

"And you believe that my niece—that Rosamund—is that woman's daughter?"

"Believe is too strong a word. I believe nothing for which I haven't positive evidence. There are accidental likenesses in the world. Your brother may have married a woman who was like Lady Chilworth. Her beauty might be his ideal. He may have worshipped the type rather than the individual in Lady Chilworth. Who knows? I am only sure of two facts

—that he admired her, and that he had been her friend in Italy before her marriage."

"Has there been no more in the papers about her escape?"

"I have seen nothing. It is a cold scent, you see; a crime of sixteen years ago. Chilworth is forgotten, the story is forgotten; nobody cares, except the asylum people, who will have to suffer the discredit of her escape."

"Five o'clock!" said Mrs. Dalrymple, as the stable clock struck the hour. "They will be waiting for me. I am deeply interested in this horrid business, Mr. Honeybill, on my poor William's account. To think that he should have all this worry and trouble in his declining years! And if it is really as you think—if Rosamund——"

She shook her head gloomily, but could say no more, for the subject of her gloomy thoughts came smiling to meet her, with Wilfred at her side.

"Do come to tea, auntie," she said. "Mr. Darrell and the Parkers want to get back by the next train, so there is no time to lose."

CHAPTER VI.

MONDAY morning's post brought Rosamund a few lines from Sir William. He regretted that he had not yet finished the business which had called him from home, so that he could not yet fix the date for his return. Then followed words of fond affection for the child he loved, with the assurance that he was well. That was all.

The letter bore the Edinburgh post-mark, but no address. Rosamund was to send her letters to the care of a solicitor in George Street.

The same post that brought her father's letter brought brighter tidings from Ronald.

"I am going south on Saturday, my angel," he wrote. "I have done my duty by the old birds—I mean the parents, not the grouse—like a Trojan. Those Trojans were famous for filial affection, you know. And I am coming on the wings of love, by the North Eastern express, next Saturday. I leave this place in the small hours, and shall be in your drawing-room—your heavenly drawing-room—late in the evening. I don't think the Governor will be sorry to see the last of me. I never shot so badly in my life, and he has made some scathing remarks about lovers. But the little mother says he was very strong himself in that line, and used to spend all his evenings at dances or theatres with her, and sit up half the night to read his briefs with a wet towel round his head.

"My loveliest and dearest, I count every minute of the gap in time 'twixt now and Saturday night."

Rosa announced her lover's return to her aunt.

"I haven't seemed to miss him so very much, have I, auntie," she asked playfully, "considering that it was our first parting?"

"No, my dear, you seem to have got on wonderfully well without him; but then you have had Wilfred—who is——"

"Ever so much cleverer than Ronnie. Don't be afraid to say so, auntie. I know all about it. But then, Ronnie is Ronnie, you see. I couldn't have him a scrap different."

"I hope you will always think the same, Rosa."

"Oh, auntie, why do you say that with a sigh? Hopes and sighs should not go together. Sighs are for regrets."

"Well, Rosa, if you want me to be frank——"

"No, no, no, don't be frank, if that means disparaging Ronnie. Can't you understand that for me he is perfect? We are each faultless for the other; and it doesn't matter a straw to us what we seem to the rest of the world, except to my dear father; and he is quite satisfied."

"You can't deprive me of the power to form an opinion, Rosa; and I shall always think that you might have made a happier choice—that you ought to have chosen a man of large mind and cultivated intelligence, a man who has work to do in the world, who had to rough it in his boyhood, who would be your strong rock in the hour of trouble, strong enough to shield you in a time of difficulty and disgrace."

"Difficulty and disgrace! What are you dreaming about, auntie? How can you talk so horridly? Yes, I know, I know," her eyes filling with tears, "trouble may come—trouble must come perhaps. Life cannot be always sunshine, as it has been for me till now. But if sorrow should come Ronald will help me to bear it. He will be my strong rock. There never was a braver spirit, never a truer heart."

She was distressed, indignant, more deeply moved than her aunt had ever seen her before.

"He is a spoilt child of fortune, Rosamund—and he is not the man I would have chosen for you, and I confess it is strange to me that you should have overlooked the worth and talents of your cousin Wilfred, in order to throw yourself away upon a feather-headed young man who has never left off acting and thinking like an undergraduate."

"My cousin Wilfred is an Admirable Crichton, I have no doubt, aunt, and I can quite understand his mother thinking him a paragon," said Rosa, her eyes flashing and her cheeks crimson with anger, "but, though I think him most estimable as a cousin, he is the last man in the world that I should ever fall in love with—and I have adored Ronald from the very beginning—I am not ashamed to confess that I worshipped him before I left off playing with my dolls, and that when I used to watch the moon from my schoolroom window I was thinking of Ronald all the time."

"Well, my dear, you have made your choice, and the future will show whether it is a wise one. I dare-say your cousin will find some nice girl who won't think him the very last man in the world she could love."

"Of course he will, aunt, myriads of girls. He is handsome, and clever, and—everything that girls like, if they don't happen to have fallen in love with some-one else when they were babies."

Rosamund's spirits had risen almost to happiness after that letter from Ronald, in spite of the trouble of her father's prolonged absence. Ronald was coming back to her, her father would come on the same day perhaps, or even sooner, and overwhelming joy would follow the poignant agony which she had borne so bravely.

Thursday was spent in London. The landau con-veyed the three ladies to Bond Street, where the coach-man was dismissed till half-past ten at night, when he was to pick them up at Queen's Hall for the home journey, Wilfred having insisted on entertaining them with a dinner in Piccadilly, and a Richter concert after-wards.

Mrs. Dalrymple left the two girls at the dressmaker's, while she went to pay a visit of charity to an old servant at Lambeth, an act of benevolence at which Octavia expressed surprise and some displeasure.

"If it's Maria, I don't think she's worth the trouble, mother."

"It is not Maria. It is a person you know nothing about—a maid I had before you were born, and I don't want any interference or advice."

"Oh, very well, mother, if you enjoy poking your way about a slum to see a person you haven't seen for over twenty years, I can't say anything against it. I hope you'll take cabs both ways, and come to no harm."

"I am not afraid of coming to any harm; and you and Rosamund will have it all your own way with Amandine."

Amandine was the dressmaker, a *protégée* of Lady Halstead's, a recent arrival in the dressmaking world, and already beginning to give herself airs.

Mrs. Dalrymple promised to be back in time to take the girls to the restaurant, and in the meantime Amandine would give them tea. She was famous for the flavour of her tea and for her semi-diaphanous bread and butter.

Rosamund's spirits were now buoyant enough to endure the tediousness of trying on inchoate skirts and bodices, and the endless discussion about details. Sir William had given her a cheque, and had told her to order the prettiest frocks and the most luxurious wraps that modern art could devise, and having never been called upon to economise about anything, she hardly knew whether things were dear or cheap. She showed considerable moderation, however, in the number of garments she ordered, and was not to be talked into extravagance by flatteries or specious representations as to the needs of a newly-married young lady.

"You are very good," she said. "But I quite know what I shall want to wear on my honeymoon tour, and afterwards. I daresay that lovely tea-gown was indispensable, as you say, for your duchess; but I am going to marry a man who hates tea-gowns."

"Gentlemen so seldom know what they like, madam; but a really beautiful creation is seldom lost upon them, and that oyster satin and orange velvet, with the marabout garniture and black pearl embroidery, would be perfect for a young lady with your splendid colouring. Such a gown would be sufficient when you did not want to dress for dinner."

"Yes, really, Rosamund, madame is right," said Octavia, who had been yawning over fashion-plates till she was in the last stage of weariness. "A tea-gown like that would be useful when you don't want to dress for dinner."

"I shall never want to dress for dinner at Tremezzo, except in a white serge skirt and a silk blouse. We shall live on the lake, and dine in the garden."

Wilfred's little dinner in Piccadilly was a success, from the white flowers on the table, which had an almost bridal air, to the illuminated ice which ended the repast. Rosamund was in good spirits; Octavia and her brother had plenty to say; and nobody noticed the acidity of Mrs. Dalrymple's countenance, partly because perhaps that soured expression had been habitual with her of late.

Rosamund and Octavia were bestowed in one cab, and Wilfred and his mother in another, to drive from Piccadilly to the Queen's Hall, where Wilfred had secured stalls in a good position.

The drive was short, but it gave time for a painful conversation between mother and son.

"Well, Wilfred, Ronald is to be back next Saturday," Mrs. Dalrymple began, "and you have lost your chance."

"What chance? For God's sake, mother, don't let me hear any more of that nonsense! What chance have I ever had with Rosamund—least of all since her engagement?"

"Most of all since then, if you had any dash and pluck, as another man with your gifts would have had. She must see your superiority to Ronald. She must feel offended with him—in her inmost heart—for leaving her. That was your opportunity. If you had proposed to her last week—when she took such pleasure in your society—if you had attacked her with something like romance and passion, instead of Ronald Halstead's commonplace—who knows? You might have taken her by storm."

"Propose to a girl who is engaged to a man I know! I'm not quite such a cad as that. Don't say any more about it, mother. You have got Rosamund's fortune on your brain. Try to forget it if you can, and take the goods the gods provide. My uncle has been very kind to us."

"And is going to turn your sister and me out of doors in three weeks."

"You may be sure he will provide a home for you!"

"A semi-detached villa perhaps, at forty pounds a year. There are thousands of them between Richmond and Hampton."

"You know better, mother. You know he will act liberally!"

"He is wrapped up in Rosamund. Everything is for Rosamund. She will have all his professional earnings, which Mr. Honeybill tells me were immense. You have been a great fool, Wilfred. If you knew as much as I do, you would think it a kindness to marry your cousin. Oh, here we are. I never have time to talk to you, at Tangley or anywhere else."

"So much the better, mother, if you must always talk rot of this kind."

The concert was delightful, but the music, the dinner, and the dressmaker's made a long day's work, and Rosamund was very tired when she arrived at

Tangley. Her aunt and cousin had slept, or seemed to sleep, through most of the journey; but she had been awake, and full of eager thought of her lover and her father, counting the hours till Ronald's return, hoping that Sir William would be with her even sooner. She looked on the hall table for letters, and carried off her own, among which there was no Scotch letter, and therefore nothing to interest her. She bade her aunt and cousin good-night at the foot of the stairs.

"I hope you are going to take some wine or something, before you go to bed, auntie," she said. "You are looking so white and tired. I'm afraid our high jinks have been too much for you. But I know Octavia will take care of you," and so she left them, glad to escape to the solitude of her pretty bedroom, where she meant to treat herself to a second—or perhaps sixth—reading of Ronald's letter.

The reading-lamp was lighted and the candles on her dressing-table. She let her maid take off her hat and exchange her smart frock for a loose cashmere gown, and then dismissed her, sinking down into her easy-chair, with a pleasant feeling of relief after a long day in company. The music was ringing in her brain, and she was worn out with the standing and trying on at Amandine's.

"Saturday, Saturday, Saturday," she said to herself. "I am like a child at school. I think I must pin up a page out of the almanack over my bed, and mark off the days as they go by. Dear old Ronald! How strange that I should be so fond of him! I suppose he really is not handsome—but it is the one face in the world for me—after my father's."

She opened her letters, trivial all of them, till she came to one addressed in an unfamiliar hand, a curious style of penmanship, stiff and laboured.

"I'm afraid it's a begging letter," she thought, of which sad documents the prosperous Miss Rayson had received a good many.

It was a type-written letter, except for the names, which were inserted in the same rigid angular writing as the address.

"You are very proud of your father, Miss Rayson, and well you may be; but you have not much reason to be proud of your mother. Have you ever asked what kind of woman she was, and when and where she died? You had better ask those questions before you marry Mr. Halstead. He might be angry if he were to discover some day that he had married the daughter of a madwoman, without being warned of his danger.

"It is a danger, you know. Madness is sometimes hereditary. I hope it won't prove so in your case—but nobody can foresee what may happen. If I were you, I wouldn't be in a hurry to marry.

"From a friend, who only knows you by sight, but who wishes to save you from future unhappiness."

What a letter! Rosamund sat with the paper spread before her in the vivid light of her reading-lamp, staring at the lines in blank wonder. She was bewildered, but at first incredulous of actual evil.

The letter was the work of some lunatic, that charge of madness against her mother—dead so many years ago, and utterly unknown to anyone in the neighbourhood of Tangley—was the wild imagining of a disordered brain. It was like madness to invent such a story. She had heard that it was a characteristic of lunacy to think other people mad.

"Some poor wretch has concocted the letter," she

told herself, "but who can it be? It must be someone who knows me, or they would not know that I am going to marry Ronald."

And then she remembered that her engagement had been announced in the *Times,* and that a local paper had expatiated upon the interesting fact, and sung praises of her beauty, and Mr. Halstead's cricket.

"It may be from an utter stranger," she reflected, "and it certainly isn't worth worrying about. I must show it to father when he comes home."

She looked at the post-mark on the envelope. Pentonville.

"Is that some place in the country?" she wondered, never having heard of that unfashionable suburb.

"Oh, how can I be so weak as to dwell upon this horrid letter? How absurd of me to be scared by a letter from a maniac."

She would show the letter to her father immediately on his return. And then suddenly she remembered that look of unspeakable pain in the dear face, years ago, when she had questioned him about her mother. Was she to re-open that old wound because of this anonymous letter from a lunatic? No, on reflection, she resolved not to trouble her father with the hateful stuff. Ronald, her husband, from whom she was to have no secrets, was the proper person to confide in. With what scornful laughter he would read the madman's warning; and how lightly he would take the matter which troubled her, in spite of her better reason.

It troubled her enough to keep away sleep. She lay awake all night, thinking of that letter, and of her motherless childhood. Such a happy childhood, so fenced round by love—but motherless. All things that concerned her mother had been a blank. She had been told nothing of that vanished existence. She had no memorial of the dead. No picture, no tress of hair, no jewel, such as other motherless girls among her friends possessed in abundance. She knew neither the scene of her mother's birth, nor the place where she lay at rest. Surely this silence must mean some dark mystery, some sorrow too deep for speech.

She started up in bed, cold and trembling, her hands clasped above her brow. Could there be a dreadful truth in that mad letter? Was the thing that had been hidden from her all her life—something horrible like that? Madness, something tragical in the past, something horrible in the present, something that made her unfit to be any man's wife——

"Oh, if it were so, if my father knew that there was the taint of madness in my veins, how could he let me engage myself to Ronald? How could he, a great physician, permit such evil?"

"No, it could not be," she told herself. The wicked letter had no foundation in fact. She could trust her father, the deep thinker, the man of science, whose life work had been the study of cause and effect in all the ills that assail mind and body.

She went downstairs at her usual hour, and made her usual round of the gardens with the stable dogs, a brace of fox terriers and an Aberdeen, before breakfast. She was resolute with herself, that this thing should not trouble her. Yet do what she would, the hateful letter went on repeating itself in her brain, like the dull, heavy ticking of an old eight-day clock. She looked at the roses, and talked to the head gardener. She played with the Aberdeen, and ran a race with the terriers; but the warm flush that the quicker movement brought to her cheek had faded before she went in at the dining-room window.

Octavia noticed her pallor.

"You must have had a bad night, Rosa," she said. "The music was too exciting for you."

"Did it keep you awake?"

"No, I am not sensitive like you. I revel in a fine orchestra, but forget all about the music directly it is over. What are we going to do to-day? The ponies must want exercise after Sunday and Monday."

Rosamund was ready to do anything her cousin liked. There was racing at Kempton Park, but they could not go alone, and Wilfred was not coming down to-day. So it ended in a long morning drive, during which Rosamund looked in upon some of the decent cottagers whom she had been allowed to visit, with *carte blanche* as to her beneficence.

Talking to one of these, a bed-ridden old man, to whom she sometimes read the Scriptures and the daily paper, she asked in a casual way:

"Have you heard of any madman living about here—or perhaps a very eccentric person, not quite mad enough to be shut up?"

No, her old pensioner, who was keen-witted, and always well posted in local news, could tell her of no such person within his ken.

On the way home she asked Octavia if she had ever heard of a place called Pentonville.

"Of course I have, Rosa. It is somewhere between King's Cross and Islington."

"Near London?"

"In London. Not three miles from Cavendish Square."

"How strange! I never heard of the place."

"No! You were brought up in cotton wool, you see. I don't suppose you ever heard of Bermondsey, or Walworth, or any of the horrid neighbourhoods. And yet people have to live and die in them."

Rosamund hardly knew how she lived through the long day, with the recurring thought of that horrible letter hanging like a cloud over every other idea. When she looked back at the day a week later it seemed to have been a feverish blank, like a dream which had left the sense of pain, but no memory of scene or circumstance.

She sat at luncheon with her aunt and cousin, and

practised all the afternoon in her den upstairs, since her piano gave her an excuse for being alone, and went down to the drawing-room at tea-time, where she found two spinster neighbours who had attached themselves to Mrs. Dalrymple. She sustained her share in the vapid small talk, and pretended to be interested in the last new inmate of the Palace, and the last matrimonial engagement which was bruited about as almost a certainty, though nobody was officially informed.

It was a long time, but at last the two ladies departed, after walking round the lawn, and admiring the roses, and being barked at by the stable terriers, who could not have resented their intrusion more vehemently had they been obvious burglars.

They were gone at last, and Rosamund was free to return to her boudoir, or wander alone in the gardens she loved. She chose the garden, sauntered across the lawn and along the terrace by the old wall, and thence into the modest little park, where some fine old beeches and an avenue of giant walnuts told of two or three centuries of peaceable occupations.

The park was divided from the outer world by an oak fence for some two-thirds of its extent, but on the side nearest the Thames, the only barrier was a sloping bank topped by a hawthorn hedge skirting a lane that led to the river. The timber here was thicker than in any other part of the grounds, and this little bit of park had a forestal air that Rosamund loved. She came here on this soft summer evening, in the yellow light of the westering sun, came to be quiet and alone, and reason herself into cheerfulness.

She had been walking to and fro under the trees for about half an hour, thinking of the anonymous letter, and of her own folly in being miserable about it, when she heard herself called by her Christian name in an unknown voice, and stopped, spell-bound, as if she had been addressed by a ghost. The face she saw looking at her across the hawthorn hedge was like a ghost's face—white, and wan, with great dark eyes, haggard and hollow, ringed round with purple shadows that made them seem unnaturally large, wild eyes, glaring at her out of a spectral countenance.

"Are you Rosamund?" asked the voice.

"Yes, that is my name. Who are you, and what do you want with me?"

"I'll tell you by-and-by. Is there a gate anywhere? Can you let me in?"

"Not till I know who you are."

"Rosamund, Rosamund! Oh, what a hard heart you must have!"

That heart was beating vehemently. A madwoman evidently; and the writer of the letter. The idea flashed into Rosamund's mind as the woman spoke.

"I cannot let a stranger into my father's park without knowing her business," she said firmly. "Have you written a letter to me?"

"Hundreds of letters, thousands of letters, but they would not send them. I have poured out my soul to you. It was a kind of comfort sometimes. And they lied to me, and said that my letters were sent. But they never were—they never were!"

"I received a very foolish and very wicked letter last night, and I believe that was from you."

"No. It is more than a week since I had a pen in my hand."

"This was a type-written letter, posted at Pentonville."

The woman looked at her with a bewildered expression.

"Let me in, Rosamund. Oh, for God's sake! I have come hundreds of miles to see you—I have lost my way, and gone to the wrong places. I am like a child in the strange, cruel world, and nobody has helped me."

The forlorn voice, the forlorn face, white and wasted, framed in dishevelled hair under a black straw-hat of an old fashion, awakened Rosamund's pity. One must be hard of heart not to pity the helplessness of lunacy, as well as the helplessness of childhood.

"Well, you shall come in and rest for a little bit and tell me your troubles," she said gently, "if you will promise to be very quiet, and to go away when you are rested."

"I promise to do anything you want me to do, if you are Rosamund," the woman answered eagerly.

"Very well. The gate is only a little way farther down the lane. You will have to wait some time while I fetch the key."

"Yes; I will wait; but don't be long."

Rosamund ran to the gardener's cottage, where keys of various gates and doors rarely used by the family were kept.

To go and return, even running the greater part of the way, occupied a quarter of an hour, and she scarcely expected that the woman would have waited for her. She was there, however, standing at the gate, with those burning eyes watching for Rosamund's approach.

She was tall and slim, with an indescribable grace of form and movement even in her weather-stained garments. She wore a grey stuff gown, the skirt draggled and stained with mud and dust, and that old-fashioned mushroom shaped straw-hat, trimmed so sparsely with a dusty black ribbon. She had no gloves, and her hands were scratched and bruised.

"Are you Rosamund?" she asked again, "really, really Rosamund?"

"Yes! I am Rosamund Rayson."

"Rosamund, *Rosa mia, la mia figlia!*" she cried, in a rapture of love, and clasped the bewildered girl to her breast, and pressed her kisses on the reluctant face, kisses from fever-parched lips that seemed to sting.

"Oh, pray do not talk this wild nonsense," Rosamund said, putting her away, as gently as she could; "you know this is mad talk, and you promised me to be very quiet. Sit down on this bench for a little while, and if you are poor I will give you some money and take you to a cottage where the people will give you a bed. But you must not talk nonsense."

"No, I will not talk nonsense. Have I not come three hundred miles to see you, and God knows how many more miles when I went to wrong places on the railway? I have been more than a week wandering about—so helpless—so frightened—knowing that my gaolers are hunting me—as hounds hunt a fox—sometimes on the scent, and sometimes off it."

"Your gaolers!" with a horrified accent.

"Yes, the madhouse people. What are they but gaolers? I was to be there all my life—a prisoner—at Her Majesty's pleasure! *His* Majesty's pleasure! They told me the old Queen was dead!"

"Oh, pray don't talk so wildly," Rosamund implored, in an agonised voice, feeling as if she was herself going mad. Those strange words, "His Majesty's pleasure," had no particular meaning for her. She did not associate them with the idea of crime or punishment.

"Sit down by me, Rosamund, sit by my side and let us talk quietly. Don't be frightened, my dearest—my dearest, my loveliest—lovelier even than my dreams of you. Only sit by my side, and let me hold your hand, and I promise to be calm and quiet."

She had seated herself on the oak bench, at Rosa's bidding, and now she took the girl's hand and drew her to her side.

Rosamund obeyed as if she had been under a spell. A curious helplessness had come upon her. No matter what this madwoman said she was obliged to listen. No matter what this woman asked, she must comply. She sat by her side, and surrendered her hand to be clasped by two fevered hands. She let the strange woman caress her, and smoothe her hair with a hand that trembled as it touched her.

"*Santo cielo,* how I have longed for this moment," she said, "for fifteen years. You were a little child then, Rosanita, so pretty, so sweet, and now you are a woman—and you stare at me like a stranger; but you are the woman that the child promised to be—lovely, and loving, and you will not thrust your mother from you!"

"My mother! Oh, why do you say these mad things, if you don't want to be thought mad, and shut up in a madhouse?" Rosamund cried imploringly, while those strange hands still held her with clinging love.

That hateful letter was in her mind, the letter that called her mother a madwoman, and here was this strange woman, who confessed herself a fugitive from a madhouse, claiming to be her mother. In the bewilderment of her brain she could only find one solution of the mystery. This woman had written the letter. This woman was under a delusion of which she—Rosamund—was the subject.

"How often must I swear that I am talking reason? Oh, child, look in my face, and see that I am telling you the truth. For years I have had your image in my mind and heart. I have hugged it—I have lived for it. I have had your pictured face to look at, year after year; a little child; a girl with streaming hair, such lovely hair; that a mother's hand never touched; a woman, exquisitely beautiful. I have known each stage of your young life—but not you; only the picture that my lips wore out with kisses—but which never gave me love for love. Year after year I longed for you, and as the years went by the longing grew wilder. *Dio,* how I wanted to see you! How my heart ached for want of you. I tried to escape once before, years ago, and was caught and taken back, and my life in that prison-house was made harder to me. I did not mind their hardness. I wanted you—only you. And then there came a chance—a drunken keeper—a secret drinker whom nobody suspected—but I knew, and I watched, and bided my time, and it came, and I was free, free to go to my beloved girl!"

Her words had come in a torrent, and now she stopped, breathless, while Rosamund gazed at her in silence, thrilled by her words, for they sounded like truth.

"Was it far away—the place you left?" she asked at last.

"In Scotland—a long way—I was able to get to the railway before anyone missed me, or they would have caught me, as they did before. The train took me to Edinburgh, and I was able to hide in a lonely place ever so far from the town, and I let a day go by, and then left late at night. I had plenty of money; gold that had been given to me to buy luxuries; but I had saved it, and hidden it against the day when I should get away. I wanted no luxuries. I only wanted you. I travelled at night—or in the early morning. I travelled third-class among poor people, in crowded carriages, and I asked no questions. It made the journey longer, for I went to wrong places; but nobody noticed me, and I got to London last night—and from London to Hampton this morning, and I have been about here all day walking up and down by the fence, watching for you. I thought you would come where I could see you, sooner or later."

"You were in Scotland," Rosamund faltered, remembering the telegram, and her father's troubled countenance.

"Fifteen years. But don't talk of it, let me forget it if I can. I wanted to see you—to be with you for a little—not to spoil your young life—no—no—love. I am not such a selfish wretch. You shall still be Sir

William Rayson's daughter. Let me live hidden somewhere near you, where I may see you now and then, if it were but to watch you pass my window in the sunshine, every day till I die. I don't think I am going to live very long, dear angel. The doctors shook their heads over me last winter. To be born in Naples, and to live through fifteen winters in Scotland! Think of that!"

"Your words sound almost like truth," said Rosamund, very gently, her hand still clasped in the woman's hand, as they sat side by side, "but this must be a dream and a delusion of yours. My mother died when I was a little child."

"Died to the world, love, and to you; but lived to long for this time. You don't believe me, *cara mia*. Will you believe if I show you your picture?" pulling a large gold locket from her bosom. "The likeness I have worn near my heart for ten years."

She opened the locket, and Rosamund saw her own photograph, taken on her ninth birthday. She had one like it among old relics in her desk.

"Yes, that is my photograph," she said, and then,

wonderingly, "can it be true? Can it be? There is a cloud over my mind when I try to look back."

"Yes, there is a cloud. You were very ill—you had a fever—and you forgot the things that happened in your infancy—the foolish things other children remember. You forgot your mother's face as well."

"I remember someone—oh, so dimly—someone who used to play with me by the sea—and pick up shells for me—and sing to me. I think I used to lie in her lap in the sunshine, looking at the blue sea, while she sang to me."

"Yes, love, yes. Do you remember the song you loved best? I have sung myself to sleep with it, sometimes; and dreamt I was back at Amalfi and you were lying on my knee."

She sang a verse of a Neapolitan love song—an air that had haunted Rosamund in her childhood. It came back to her as the woman sang.

"Yes, yes, that is the song. I remember it all now. I remember eyes like yours—and I believe you are telling me the truth. Oh mother, mother, mother, to think that we should have been parted all these years! I thought you were dead."

"I have been dead," the other answered, gloomily. "Ah, child, you cannot imagine what this death is like —not to lie asleep in the dark earth, knowing neither sorrow nor pain—but to drag on life that is but half alive, day after day, year after year, every day the same as yesterday, every year the same as last year—a prisoner among hard faces—and bare walls. I had nothing, *Rosa mia,* nothing but my dreams of you, and the hope of this day."

"Mother, mother!"

This time it was Rosamund whose lips were pressed against the other woman's wasted cheek. She no longer shrank from her embrace, no longer looked at her in blank amazement. Love had conquered, irresistible, invincible: the love of a mother who had hungered for her child's affection.

"Oh, mother, why were they so cruel as to keep you from me? It could not be my father's fault. I know how he grieved for you. I saw the sorrow in his face years ago, when I questioned him about my mother."

There was a pause. The woman looked at her

thoughtfully, and then answered very slowly, as if she were weighing her words.

"No, William Rayson has always been kind. He is a good man."

Rosamund did not press the question. The possibilities of the case were passing rapidly through her mind as she sat by the woman's side, her mother, as she fully believed now. The passion of the woman, so thrilling, so intense, the old melody dimly remembered from childhood, and something familiar in the eyes and expression of the haggard countenance, all faint and blurred like a half-remembered dream—these things had gone far to convince her of the stranger's truth. This was not a lunatic or an impostor. This was her mother.

And for the sad fate, the long years of imprisonment in a madhouse, she could account only by the idea, that, rational as her mother's speech appeared at this moment, she was of unsound mind, subject to hallucinations, a danger to herself and others, and needing restraint. It was painful to think that this was so, but knowing her father as she did, Rosamund could not for an instant credit that there had been cruel injustice done to her father's wife.

What was she to do? What was her duty to this desolate wanderer, who hung upon her with such intensity of love? She sat for some minutes lost in thought, bewildered, weighed down by the burden that had fallen on her, the dreadful responsibility of this woman's fate, this broken, unhappy life, which must needs be dear to her.

"Oh, mother, mother, what are we to do?" she cried despairingly.

The woman had been watching her countenance, seeing doubt and anxiety there, reading her thoughts almost.

"Rosamund," she cried, with a sudden grip upon the girl's arm, "Rosamund, you won't let them take me back—back to that prison—that living grave? Oh, you can't be such a cruel daughter—my child, the babe I nursed, and cherished, and worked for, when there was no one to help. You won't give me back to my gaolers? If you could do that you must have a heart of stone."

"No, no, no! I will do whatever is best for you. I will do whatever can make you happiest. Poor, poor mother! God will show us a way. No, no, you sha'n't go back. Father will help us."

"Sir William! No, no, Rosa, he must not know where I am. He would take me back to the madhouse. He would call it duty. You must hide me from all the world—hide me somewhere—anywhere—in any hovel—where I shall be a free woman, and where I can see you—now and then. I don't ask for much, *carissima*—I have no right to ask—only to be free from bonds—and to see you sometimes."

"I will try," Rosamund said, clasping her hands before her face. "I will try to think of something. Let me think, mother."

CHAPTER VII.

THE sun was sinking, the dusk was thickening under the beeches and hawthorns, and Rosamund knew that it was time she should be in the house, dressing for dinner, and that if she delayed her return much longer people would be sent to look for her. And she had this helpless wanderer to provide for, and only minutes in which to find a safe shelter with people whom she could trust.

A deliberate choice was impossible. At any moment the messenger might come, a footman, or her own maid, to look for her, and that would mean discovery.

The gardeners were gone. There was no one about in the grounds. They could get away unobserved if they went at once. But where could they go?

There was only one possible shelter near at hand. One of the gardeners had an invalid wife for whom Rosamund had done a great deal, and whom Sir William had snatched from the gates of death. Husband and wife had a grateful affection for the girl who had devoted her time and care, as well as bounteous gifts, to the humble sick-room. Rosamund was sure that these people would do anything in the world to serve her. They would be staunch, come what might. She could trust this poor fugitive with them. The cottage was in the lane, not more than five minutes' walk from the gate, a cottage in a garden of half an acre, hidden behind the belt of elms on that side of the park. There could hardly be a safer spot.

"Come, mother, I have thought of a place; but we must be quick if you don't want to be found here," Rosamund said resolutely.

A far-off church clock chimed the first quarter after seven as she spoke.

"I will go anywhere with you, Rosa, anywhere," said her mother, following her through the gate.

Rosamund locked it on the outside, and put the key in her pocket.

"It is only a cottage," she said, "but the people will be kind, and we can think of something better afterwards. You will not tell them who you are, or where you have come from, will you, mother?"

"No, no, *cara mia,* I will be as secret as the grave."

Mrs. Clark, the gardener's wife, was sitting at needlework near the open window, profiting by the last of the daylight, her lamp ready to be lighted on the round table, and her husband's supper laid on a spotless tablecloth. It was one of those cottage interiors which make sentimental people despise fine houses, everything of a meticulous cleanliness, and of a rustic prettiness that composed itself into a cabinet picture.

Rosamund explained briefly what she wanted. Susan, the grown-up daughter, was in service, and Susan's room was empty. Would Mrs. Clark let this lady occupy it for a night or two, and would she make her as comfortable as possible, and let nobody know of her presence there?

"The lady has been very unfortunate, you see, Mrs. Clark; and she has enemies who are anxious to get her back into their power, so I have undertaken the care of her. I know you will do as much as this to oblige me."

"Oh, Miss Rayson, I hope you know I would do a great deal more than that, and more again. I could never do enough for one that did so much for me. Susan's room is quite ready. I keep it aired and dusted always—for my daughter is in service in London, ma'am," turning to the stranger, "and her mistress lets her stay the night with us when she has her holiday, and go back early next morning. The room is very small, as Miss Rayson knows, but I'll answer for its being clean, and as comfortable as such a room can be."

"It will do very well for me, whatever it is," said the wanderer, sinking into a chair, very white in the glare of the lamp, which Mrs. Clark had just lighted.

"And would not the lady like some supper? There's a bit of cold boiled pork, and a fresh lettuce, and I could make some tea."

"Yes, I daresay Mrs. Smith would like some tea. The lady's name is Smith. And you will be sure to remember that no one is to be told anything about her, no one at the house least of all. My aunt and cousins don't know her; and they would not understand her troubles. So I rely on you to keep our secret. Mrs. Smith is my friend, my very dear friend."

She bent down to kiss the pale forehead as she spoke.

"And now I must go, or they will be looking for me. *A rivederci, Madre mia.*"

Another kiss and she was gone, and Mrs. Smith let her head sink forward on her clasped hands and sobbed aloud.

"Oh, ma'am, I'm so sorry to see you give way. Do let me get you a cup of tea," said the gardener's wife, busy with the neat little canister and the Rockingham teapot, as she spoke, "and I hope you'll be able to eat something, for I'm sure you are over-tired. And while you are taking a bit of supper, I'll go upstairs and make your bed, and I think you'll find it comfortable."

Rosamund ran for the greater part of her way home through the little park and gardens. It was ten minutes to eight when she arrived breathless in her own room, where her maid was waiting for her, with the evening frock laid out.

"I was getting quite anxious about you, miss!"

"It was foolish of me to stop so long. I went to see one of the cottagers," Rosamund said carelessly.

She was in the drawing-room soon after eight, where her aunt received her in silence, apparently absorbed in the evening paper.

"Where have you been hiding yourself since tea, Rosa?" asked Octavia. "I was looking for you to practise our Wagner duet."

"I have been in the park, trying to cure a headache with a long walk. I did not like to stay away from dinner; but I shall go to bed directly after."

"Poor Rosa! You should not have come downstairs if your head aches. You ought to have gone to bed and let me read you to sleep. The last novel from Mudie's would be as good as sulphonel."

"It's very kind of you to think of it, Octavia, but I shall be better quite quiet after dinner."

"You are looking awfully white and ill. Mother, don't you think Rosa looks ill? Oughtn't we to send for Dr. Manders?"

Mrs. Dalrymple put down her paper and looked at her niece.

"Yes, you are looking ill—or tired, Rosamund. Would you like to see the doctor?"

"Not for worlds. I have only a headache that will be gone to-morrow. Pray don't trouble about me, auntie."

The three ladies sat down to dinner, but only one

of the three can be said to have dined, for Mrs. Dalrymple ate very little more than her niece, who ate scarcely anything. Indeed, Rosamund's heart was beating so violently that she thought other people must hear it, and her brain was in a tumult of hurrying thoughts.

Was the story true? Had she been deluded after all, the dupe of a madwoman? What proof had been given her of that wild assertion? On the strength of tears and kisses, of impassioned words, and of an old tune remembered from childhood, she had believed this strange woman to be the mother whose existence had been hidden from her. The evidence was of the slightest, and yet she believed the story. She believed in spite of herself. Something of days long forgotten, blotted out by the fever that had put her life in peril, had come back to her with the touch of that tremulous hand, with the look of unspeakable love in that grief-worn countenance.

These thoughts were in her mind as she sat at dinner, and tried to join in the feeble flow of small talk which Octavia kept up, Mrs. Dalrymple seeming almost as absent-minded as her niece.

At last the grapes and pears had been handed, and the wine had been offered and refused, and the evening meal—which is so gay and pleasant when all things are happy with those who sit at the board, and such a spectral feast when care broods over the company—came to an end, and Rosa bade her aunt and cousin good-night, and went straight to her own room.

She let her maid bring her some tea, and dismissed her for the night, and then sat at her lamplit table, thinking what she was to do for this dear wanderer, for this woman for whom her heart was pleading with irresistible force.

Could there be a charge more sacred, a duty more direct? The mother whose life for the last fifteen years had been one long misery, was dependent upon her for rescue from that wretched existence, for freedom and peaceful days.

Mad? Yes, doubtless she had once been mad, and it had seemed to Sir William Rayson that the only cure was the restraint of an asylum. And then when improvement, or even cure came, he had by some means been kept ignorant of the change; he had left his wife in that sepulchre of the living, had believed that she was still among the dead-alive, the lost souls who have no place in the world where they were once happy and gay.

How beautiful she must have been, this poor mother, in the days of her youth! How sad to think of the slow decay of beauty in those fifteen years, unmarked, unregretted!

Rosamund did not doubt that her father had gone to Scotland on a summons from the lunatic asylum, and that he had been employed since in the endeavour to trace the fugitive. What would he do if he came home and found her here? Would he disbelieve in her cure—deem it his painful duty to give her back to her gaolers? She herself had declared that it would be so. And could the daughter who loved and pitied her, subject her to the hazard of that cruel doom?

It might be that she was subject to acute attacks of mania, and was sane and rational as she seemed now in the intervals of her malady.

"If I take charge of her, if I devote my life to her, as I ought to do, I must be prepared for such a calamity. I must guard her and protect her in case of a relapse. I feel that I can do it. Yes, with God's help, I can do it."

This was the burden that had been laid upon her. She took it up willingly, for it was all that life seemed to offer her since the revelation of her mother's insanity. The writer of the anonymous letter had shown her her duty. She was no wife for Ronald Halstead. That dream was ended. She took out his last letter—his joyous letter announcing his return, and kissed it, dry-eyed, broken-hearted.

"Thank God I have something to do, somebody to take care of," she thought. "I should go mad if it were not for that."

"I should go mad!" A thrill of horror ran through her veins as she shaped the words. Was there not the taint of insanity in those veins, hereditary, inevitable? And this feeling of despair, this wild anguish as she thought of her lover—hers no more. Was it but a forerunner of the doom that must come to her sooner or later?

But, meanwhile, if she could save her mother from the horrors of the asylum, and possibly make the cure complete by her ministering love, it would be something done.

And then, even in her despair, she remembered that she would be better off than that innumerable army of good women who have given up earthly love for Christ's sake, who have put a barrier between their lives and all human joys. She would have her mother, she would have this warm, earthly love close at hand, to toil for and to hope for. She would have this immediate recompense for her sacrifice.

And her father, that fond and indulgent father, whom she adored, she was going to desert him for an indefinite time, to sever herself from that sheltering love, that ideal home, for the sake of this unhappy mother, whose claims seemed to her irresistible, the claim of utter helplessness, the claim of unhappy years, suffered perhaps uselessly and unjustly, by a victim who had been treated as a lunatic after the recovery of her reason, or whose intervals of sanity had brought no alleviation of suffering. She could not understand how so wise and good a man as her father could suffer this injustice to be done, but she felt sure that there had been injustice, and she felt that it was her mission to make amends.

She sat up late into the night, making her plans,

calculating her means, and packing two light bags with necessaries, one for her mother and one for herself. Never before had she been called upon to plan and act for herself. She had lived like a child in a garden, where all things are beautiful and safe. But her spirit rose to the occassion, and she felt equal to grapple with difficulties. Her only fear was that she might not plan her course wisely.

Her scheme was to take her mother to some remote neighbourhood, where no one would be likely to trace them, some dull street in that thickly populated outer London, a street of humble lodging-houses, where people come and go without observation, a floating multitude, who come into the world, and leave it, uncared for and unrecorded except by a line in a census paper. She knew of such a neighbourhood, which she had visited once with her father, at the opening of a workmen's coffee-house and concert-room, to the building of which Sir William had contributed largely.

She would take her mother to St. Mary's Town, a neighbourhood which no one in search of her would be likely to think of, rather than to some rustic village where their arrival and their every movement would be watched and commented upon. It was not a pleasant region to choose for a mental patient whose lasting cure she hoped for; but her mother's safety was of the first importance. She wanted time before her father found his fugitive wife, time to calm those agitated spirits so that when she could venture to bring husband and wife together she could say, "You see, father, there can be no more question of my mother going back to the asylum. She is no more mad than you or I."

This was the hope that sustained her in her self-sacrifice. She renounced her lover for ever, hardened her mind against the thought that she could never be his wife, but she thought of her separation from her father as only a temporary ordeal. So soon as she could get some experienced doctor to pronounce her mother of sound mind the necessity for concealment would be at an end.

She had plenty of money, for she had spent less than half of the liberal sum that Sir William had given her for her *trousseau*. She wrote to Amandine cancelling all orders which had not been put in hand;

and then came the harder task of writing to her father, and to Ronald. That letter, the hardest of all, she left till the last.

"Dearest Father, best and kindest of men," she began, "I am taking a desperate step, which may make me seem ungrateful and unloving to you, who are dearer to me than words can say. The poor mother, escaped from her cruel prison, has come to me for help and pity. She speaks with horror of the place she has left, and is full of fear lest she should be taken back there. She thinks that you would send her back, and throws herself upon me, her daughter, to save her. I know how good you are—how kind—how just—but you might think it your duty to place her under restraint, not believing, as I do, in her cure.

"In this fear, I am taking upon myself to care for her and shelter her—for some time to come, till I can be assured that she is restored to perfect mental health. I shall keep aloof from everyone I know, even from you, my dear, kind father, lest, if you found her with me, before her mind has grown calm and sound, as I feel convinced it will in peace and freedom, you might send her back to that joyless prison-house where she has suffered so long.

"I am doing this, dear father, because it seems to me the thing I must do, after long and deep thought. You are first, you will always be first, in my love and reverence, and I shall count the hours till I can come back to you. But all idea of ever being Ronald's wife has ended with my knowledge of my mother's affliction. I shall never marry. I should think it a crime to bring upon any man the risk of such a sorrow as you have suffered. In your indulgent love you must have shut your eyes to that danger, or you would not have allowed me to engage myself to my poor Ronald. I am writing to him to-night, to cancel our engagement, without giving any reason. You will do all you can, dear father, by your sympathy and kindness, to reconcile him to our separation.

"Good-bye, till I can write and tell you that my mother is cured. Have no fear for our safety. I have plenty of money to carry on life for a considerable time in the simple way that will suit us best. This responsibility has made me feel ten years older, and

I believe I am equal to my task.—Ever your fond daughter,

"ROSA."

Her letter to Ronald was very brief:

"DEAREST,—Something has happened which changes the whole plan of my life, and which compels me to part from you for ever. Forgive me, if you can, and believe that it is no caprice of my own, no lessened love for you, that makes me forego the happy life we were to have spent together. Forget me as soon as you can; my prayer will be that you may find a happier woman than your loving and sorrowful

"ROSAMUND."

Her tears came as she wrote—tears and passionate sobs, but she let no drop blister the page. She enclosed this brief farewell in her letter to her father, trusting to his discretion to give it to Ronald at the fittest moment.

She wrote a line to her aunt, to the effect that she was leaving home for reasons which she had explained to her father. This letter she left on the mantelpiece in her room; the other she posted later.

She was up before anyone else in the house next morning, and made her toilet unassisted, then went noiselessly downstairs, and out into the garden with her two bags, found an under-gardener, and made him carry them to Mrs. Clark's cottage. He had carried things there before, comforts of food and clothing, during the woman's long illness, and except for the early hour there was nothing singular in the proceeding.

At the cottage door Rosamund gave him a sovereign, and enjoined him to tell no one where he had carried the bags, or that he had seen her that morning; and that was the last that was seen of Sir William Rayson's daughter at Tangley, before his return, which happened, unannounced, late on the next evening.

CHAPTER VIII.

SIR WILLIAM found Rosamund's letter among his other letters. Stunned by the shock of hearing that his daughter had disappeared mysteriously on the previous morning, he stood on his desolate hearth with her letter open in his hand, while his sister watched him with anxious eyes. He looked up and encountered that searching gaze, which irritated his strained nerves.

"Have you told me everything, Margaret?" he asked. "For God's sake keep nothing back. This is a matter of life and death, remember."

"Is it likely I should keep anything back?" Mrs. Dalrymple asked, with an aggrieved air. "Rosamund's disappearance was quite as great a shock to Octavia and me as it has been to you. Wilson rushed into my room before I was up, bringing Rosa's letter. She had taken the morning tea to her room at half-past seven as usual, and had found the room empty. Wilson and I searched Rosa's bedroom and boudoir for any clue. Everything was in its place except two light bags, that had been taken out of a closet, some linen and some things from the dressing-table. The jewel case was in the safe, of which Wilson has a duplicate key. Rosa had only lain down on the outside of the bed, and must have left the house before a creature was up. You know how late the servants are. But Rosa said in her letter that she had explained her departure to you."

"Yes, she has given me her reasons. There is nothing blameworthy in what she is doing. It is only very foolish. She has acted precipitately, on the first impulse of her loving heart," said Sir William, almost as if thinking aloud.

"It is a most extraordinary affair, but I am not going to ask any questions," Mrs. Dalrymple began.

"Don't!" said her brother; "for I could not answer them."

"Shall I order some dinner for you? There were some partridges that were hardly touched—or if you would prefer cutlets——"

"Dinner!" said Sir William angrily. "I don't feel

as if I could ever eat again. Tell Grant to take some whisky and soda to the library. I shall want nothing more to-night."

"Is there really nothing we can do for you, William?"

"Nothing, except leave me alone. There are times when that is a service. Good night."

He was gone, and his sister sat down by the lamp-lit table, covered with books and periodicals, which she had been making a pretence of reading since dinner, while Octavia amused herself at the piano.

She had looked forward to her brother's return with a vague terror, as of something that might bring peril to herself. The crisis had come upon her suddenly, and it had passed and left her unharmed. She breathed more freely than she had done for some time. The sense of relief was a kind of happiness.

Octavia had got herself out of the way when she heard her uncle's voice in the hall. She came back now, after hearing him retire to the library.

"Well, mother, how did uncle take Rosa's flight?"

"More calmly than I expected; but he is very much cut up. Of course, he will have it that she's not to blame. The wildest thing she can do is only worthy of praise."

"It must be nice to have such a father. Well, it's a profound mystery. It doesn't seem possible that she could have gone away with a lover, for she has hardly ever been out of my sight since we have been here, and she adored Ronald Halstead with an idiotic devotion."

Sir William sat up late that night, and left home next morning. It was Saturday morning, and Ronald was expected at Tangley that night—Ronald who would go there light of heart, full of joyful expectation, to find his sweetheart vanished. The thought of his despair wrung the elder man's heart.

He telegraphed from London to Sir Henry Halstead, at Braeside:

"Great trouble has come upon me. Can you come to London? Reply to Athenæum."

He waited at his club for the reply, which came late in the afternoon:

"Just home from shooting. Will be at Tangley to-morrow afternoon. Sorry to hear of trouble.—HALSTEAD."

It was past eight when Sir William came home that evening. His sister and niece had been waiting dinner, a fact which he was too pre-occupied to notice by an apology. He had spent a busy afternoon, taking measures for tracing Rosa and her companion, but in his total ignorance of what direction the fugitives might take, and in his desire to avoid publicity of any kind, the chances of finding them were slight. He put the case into the hands of a private detective of unquestionable respectability, charging him to act with the utmost discretion. The difficulty of the case was increased by the fact that Rosamund had taken so little personal property with her.

Two women of the ages of mother and daughter, both singularly handsome, and having a certain likeness to each other, were to be hunted for within an unknown area. They might have crossed the Channel; they might have gone to some remote country village; they might have stayed in London.

"That would be our worst chance, sir," said the detective. "If they've crossed, or if they've gone to some out-of-the-way hole in the country, I'm pretty sure to find them; but if they stick in this wilderness I may be a long time about it."

"Criminals are found, even in the wilderness," said Sir William. "Criminals almost always do the wrong thing. They are eaten up with self-consciousness, and their vanity gives them away. They think everybody is watching them, and they get the hunted look that arouses suspicion."

A telegram addressed to Miss Rayson was brought to Sir William a few minutes before nine. It was from Ronald, and despatched at eight o'clock from the last stopping-place of the Scotch express:

"Too late to come to Tangley to-night. Shall be with you before breakfast to-morrow."

Ronald had travelled by the day train, and his father would follow through the night. Sir William wrote a telegram to be sent from Hampton at the earliest possible hour next morning:

"Don't come to Tangley. I am going to Hyde Park Gardens by first available train.—WILLIAM RAYSON."

This message, in a sealed envelope, was given to the butler to be taken to the post-office immediately. Telegrams were despatched on Sunday mornings between seven and eight.

"I shall face them both together, father and son," thought William Rayson, and then with his elbow on the table and his head leaning on his clenched hand he gave himself up to despairing thoughts. The palace of his peace, the sanctuary which he had built for his declining years, was shattered, his daughter's love-dream was broken, the bond of friendship, the quiet growth of a lifetime, was loosened perhaps for ever. He saw no ray of light, no far-off star of hope, along the dark and troubled road.

CHAPTER IX.

THE Sunday morning train from Hampton landed Sir William Rayson at the Royal Oak before eleven, in time for him to have heard any one of the famous preachers who were starred in the Saturday papers. The journey, with its change of trains at Richmond, and its endless stoppages between Hammersmith and Paddington, had seemed excruciatingly slow to a traveller whose brain was working at racing pace. Poor Ronald! Oh, to have it over and done with, to see the blow struck, and the brave young spirit stand up against it! To be able to give all his mind to the task of finding Rosamund, and providing for the safety of that other fugitive who had flung the burden of her tragical fate upon him!

Sir Henry Halstead was in his library. There had been time enough for him to make his usual careful toilet, and eat his breakfast, while Sir William was chafing at the stations on the Metropolitan. Ronald was with his father, pale and anxious, starting to his feet and coming to Sir William in an agitated way before the butler could announce the visitor.

"Why wasn't I to go to Tangley? There is something wrong, I know. Rosa is ill—dangerously ill!" he said, gaspingly.

"No, it is not that. There is trouble for you, Ronald, but not that."

"What is it then? It must be about Rosa, or you would not have forbidden me to go to her. It must be something serious or you would not have sent for my father."

"Ronald, for God's sake be quiet," said Sir Henry. "Sit down, Rayson," shaking his hand fervently, "and tell us your trouble—our trouble, for we are of one family. Rosamund is well, you say?"

Sir William nodded affirmatively.

"Then nothing can be ill. We can face anything else. Come, my dear old friend, why did you send for me? Is it money troubles? Is it the damning itch of modern times? Have you poured the earnings of a lifetime down some rotten gold-mine, and beggared yourself and Rosa? Don't be downhearted. That won't break Ronnie's heart, or mine. I have enough for both of them."

"No, Halstead, it isn't money. It does me good to hear you talk like that; but, of course, I knew you were the right metal. It has nothing to do with money. I am rich, and Rosamund will be rich, come what may."

"That's a good hearing! But if it isn't sickness, or loss of fortune, what is the trouble?"

"Give me time," said Sir William. "It's rather a long story, and not an easy one for me to tell."

"Is it for my ear alone? Shall Ronald go?"

"No, no, Ronald is to hear every word. I don't want to tell the story twice. You remember our party at George Chilworth's shooting lodge?"

"I'm not likely to forget it. A tragedy like that sticks in a man's memory."

"You helped to save Lady Chilworth from the gallows."

"I did my best. But it was your evidence, as a famous doctor, that saved her. If you hadn't made the jury believe in her insanity, she must have swung."

"Well, she was saved—as we call it—kept alive at any rate—and she bore her life, miserable as it was, for fifteen years. She made several attempts to escape in the course of those years, and made her condition a good deal worse by those attempts. That she failed was natural, that she should have ever made the attempt was wonderful, seeing the difficulty of it; but she has a daughter whom she adores, and that gave her a desperate courage. She made another attempt three weeks ago and succeeded."

"Only to be caught and taken back, I suppose," said Halstead, while Ronald stood with his back to the mantelpiece, motionless and intent, wondering what on earth Lady Chilworth's movements could have to do with the trouble at Tangley, that trouble which was keeping him from his idolised Rosa.

He had heard the story of the Chilworth murder, and had forgotten it, being an essentially modern young man, with mind and body always fully occupied by the work of to-day, and seldom troubling himself about things that belonged to the past.

"No, she has not been taken back. While I was in Scotland helping in the search for her, fearing that she had made away with herself, she was on her way to London; and she appeared at Tangley last Thursday. She appealed to Rosamund for help and protection, and they are now together."

"At Tangley?" Ronald asked eagerly.

"No, Rosamund feared that I should send the unhappy woman back to the asylum, and she has taken her away."

"What folly!" exclaimed Sir Henry. "You will put a stop to this, of course. Where have they gone?"

"I don't know."

"You don't know! Your daughter is with an escaped lunatic, and you don't know where she is?"

"It is terrible, but it is the truth. Those two women are hiding somewhere; and I don't know when they may be found. I have put the matter in the hands of the best man I could hear of, a retired detective recommended by the people at Scotland Yard. Whatever can be done will be done; and I have the utmost confidence in Rosamund. I know what a lucid mind she has. I know her good sense and courage. I have trained her, Halstead—my beloved girl—and I know what she is."

Tears were in his eyes, and he was very near breaking down; but he fought against his weakness, and held himself bravely through this bitter hour.

"But what took that woman to Tangley? What made her throw herself upon your daughter for protection?" asked Sir Henry.

His friend paused for a few moments, with bent head and thoughtful brow, before replying. Then lifting that grave white head, and looking Sir Henry full in the face, he said:

"She threw herself upon her own daughter—the child whose image has never been absent from her mind in fifteen miserable years—the child she idolised."

"Her daughter—her child! Are you mad, Rayson?"

"No—I have been mad, perhaps, to keep this secret from you and Ronald. I have done wrong—but—but I love this girl so dearly. I know how pure and perfect a creature she is; and I feared that if you knew she was that unhappy woman's daughter, you would imagine some evil taint, some hereditary weakness."

"Imagine!" cried Sir Henry, white with anger. "Imagine some evil taint! The child of a homicidal lunatic!"

"She was not a lunatic—she has never been a lunatic!"

"You dare tell me that, Rayson—you who swore she was mad when she fired the shot."

The two faces looked at each other, one convulsed with rage, the other calm, but pale as ashes.

"She was mad—at that moment. She fired that shot in a moment of fury so intense that there is no other name for it but madness. She had been told that her child was in peril of death, and she wanted to go to her. Her heart was bursting with grief, her mind was distracted with apprehension—and her husband, that human icicle, refused to let her leave his house. She snatched up the pistol. She threatened him. He was obdurate, laughed at her fury; and she fired."

"Yes, I remember the story she told us—in one of her lucid intervals. What a Jesuit you are, Rayson! Homicidal madness! You swore to that, I think—you, a specialist in mental cases."

"I swore to a condition of madness when the shot was fired."

"And you talked learnedly of recurrent mania, cited cases, and authorities—you gave me my cue—and between us we befogged a Scotch jury, and saved the woman's life. But I was her advocate. I was not in the witness-box—I was not upon oath. You perjured yourself, William Rayson, you swore to a lie to save the life of your mistress—and then you lied tacitly to Ronald and me, and would have imposed that woman's daughter upon us—the daughter of Chilworth's wife, and your cast-off mistress."

"You wrong her and me, Halstead. I am not a scoundrel, and she was true as steel. She never belonged to any man but George Chilworth, who ought to have married her before her child was born, and who did not marry her till four years later, when he came into his fortune."

"Then Rosamund is not your daughter?" exclaimed Sir Henry.

"My daughter by adoption only. She was an orphan—homeless, penniless, for her father left no will, and she had no legal claim on his estate. I took her to my heart then, a sick child, not five years old, her memory of infancy impaired by a severe attack of scarlet fever; and I have held her in my heart ever since, and shall so hold her till I die, the dearest thing this earth contains for me. I suppose I did wrong in keeping this secret from you and your son, Halstead; but I knew my girl, and knew that all England could not find a sweeter creature to bless a good man's life. I was not afraid of the result."

"No, sir, you did no wrong," Ronald said, giving Sir William his hand. "What difference could my dear love's parentage make? I know, as you know, her lovely nature, her noble mind. I know how good God has been in giving me her love. Whatever her mother may have been——"

"She murdered her husband, Ronald; please don't forget that detail. It is not a bagatelle. Come, Rayson, you and I are old friends, and have been good friends, but you have used me badly, and if you think I shall countenance my son's marriage with Lady Chilworth's daughter——"

"Your son has a will of his own, sir, and must use

it when the happiness of his life is at stake," Ronald interrupted hotly.

"There need be no quarrel," said Sir William in his low, grave voice—that voice which had so often pronounced the death-sentence, not to the patient, for it was rarely that he deemed it his duty to destroy hope, but to the patient's heart-broken kindred—"there need be no quarrel, Halstead. My daughter cancels her engagement to your son. I have her letter to Ronald."

He handed the little folded note, which Ronald snatched with a shaking hand.

"Oh, Sir William, can you think I shall abide by this?" he said, when he had read Rosamund's farewell. "Do you think I shall submit to be cast off? I swear that if there is any power in honest love, Rosamund shall be my wife. I swear that if I fail in bringing her back to me, no other woman shall ever fill her place."

"You will have to find her first," said Sir William, "and you will have to reckon with her will, and her sense of duty. I came here to tell you that your engagement was ended, and to ask your forgiveness for having deceived you."

"Oh, Sir William, I have nothing to forgive. I can understand that, loving her as you do, you could hardly bear to remember that she is not really your daughter, still less to tell anyone her mother's story. And if you thought any scientific bosh about hereditary madness would scare me—me, her lover, knowing every look in the exquisite face, every thought in the clear, calm brain—if you thought I should be frightened because her mother was an ill-used wife, and had the misfortune to put a bullet into a tyrannical husband—I daresay she only meant to frighten him, and pulled the trigger unawares— you must have a very low estimate of a modern lover."

"I doubt if all modern lovers are up to your form, Ronald."

Sir Henry Halstead had been slowly pacing the room, his habit when in perplexed thought. His footsteps had worn a track of shabbiness across the Turkey carpet between one oak bookcase and another—the utmost length of a spacious room. He stopped suddenly in front of his old friend.

"Rayson, you loved that woman! I suspected it under Chilworth's roof, I am sure of it now."

"Yes," William Rayson answered, with a sigh. "I loved her. I loved her from the hour these eyes first looked upon her in the shabby music-hall at Naples—when Chilworth and I were fellow travellers, and strolled in, curious to see what a Neapolitan *café chantant* was like. No, Ronald, Rosa's mother was not born in the purple. She was the daughter of a shop-keeper, who had died bankrupt and penniless, and left her to earn her bread how she could. She was only the loveliest woman I ever saw, with a superb contralto voice, and an extraordinary capacity for doing anything she wanted to do. We saw her shoot at a mark that night, I remember. Could either of us think that one day the mark would be Chilworth's heart? Yes, Harry, I loved her, I loved her! She was the only woman I ever cared for after I was five-and-twenty; and I have not looked upon a woman with a lover's eyes since I knew that she could never be my wife."

"You would have married her off-hand, I suppose," said Halstead, with a touch of contempt.

"I loved her too well to have any baser thought."

"And she refused you?"

"Before I had time to ask her, Chilworth had spoilt

my chance. He took her away from Naples, and when I met him in London six months after, he would tell me nothing about her, except that she was safe, and properly provided for. He was a poor man, he said, but he was not a brute, and he would not let her starve. I went back to Naples in the following autumn, and did not rest till I found her, in a cottage at Amalfi, with her baby, living as peasants live, but with a self-respect that kept her from any intercourse with her neighbours. She was devoted to her child, lived only for that, and she seemed happy. She was lovelier than ever in that serene and retired life. I know no picture of the Virgin Mother that surpasses the tranquil beauty of her countenance as she sat on the beach with her baby on her knees.'"

"She did not think herself deserted by her lover?"

"No. She was resigned to his absence. She was able to live, and her child filled her life. 'He says he may want me to live in England some day,' she told me. 'I hope English air will suit Rosa.'"

"And you loitered in Amalfi, I suppose?" said Halstead, sharply. "You played the old, sad, bad game of the moth round the candle."

"Yes, I stayed. She gave me her friendship. I knew nothing better in life than to be in her company. She never knew that I loved her. I was useful to her, and the child loved me, as babies love the first strong man who will carry them about and play with them. Mariana thought I was an adorer of infancy. She never suspected that I loved her child because it was hers. Don't despise me, Halstead. You don't know what a great unhappy love means for a man who has passed the meridian of his life. Fate smiled upon your love, and gave you a charming wife for the asking. Now can you understand? Yes, I loved her always, and knew how to respect her and myself. She never has had an inkling of my secret. She has always been able to lean upon me—in her joy and in her despair, as the one friend she could trust."

"You are a good fellow, Rayson, and there is very little I would not do to prove my friendship for you—except to approve of my son's marriage with the daughter of a murderess. Mad or sane can make little difference. Lady Chilworth's daughter is no wife for Ronald."

"I hope I'm not an undutiful son," said Ronald,

his pale face fixed as stone, "but in this business I must take my own line. You can turn me out of your house, and cut me off with a shilling; though I think you won't do either—but I belong to Rosamund, and our marriage depends upon no will but hers. And now, Sir William, will you be kind, and let me help you to look for her? I shall be fit for nothing else on earth till she is found."

"My dear boy, I'm afraid there's very little for us to do but to wait and hope. I've put the matter into professional hands, and I hope she may be traced speedily. I shall put an advertisement in the *Times*, urging her to communicate with me, but, if you read that," handing him Rosamund's letter, "you will see that for her mother's sake she may hide herself from us for some time to come. She knows nothing yet, remember, of her mother's crime. She thinks of her only as a fugitive from a lunatic asylum. Her mother may tell her that terrible story, perhaps. She may not be spared that blow."

"You think her mother is sane now?"

"Yes, Ronald. I believe she has been sane for years, though the medical authorities who have seen her from time to time and the house-surgeon at the asylum have doubted her sanity."

"You have seen her sometimes?"

"No year has passed in which I have not seen her. I was the only link between her and the life outside her prison walls. I could talk to her of her child."

"And you never took Rosamund to see her?"

"No. I would not spoil Rosa's life by the knowledge of that dark history. I wanted her existence to be cloudless. Her mother had sinned, and could not escape the penalty of her sin. She had no right to share it with her innocent child. I, who so loved her, was hard with her, cruel, perhaps, when Rosa's happiness was at stake. Good-bye, Halstead, good-bye, Ronald," taking up his hat and stick, and moving towards the door. "You shall hear from me if there is any news."

"Let me go down to Tangley with you, Sir William. I shall be a shade happier there."

"No, no, Ronald. I have no right to foster an attachment which your father will not sanction."

"My father has no voice in this matter, sir. I am his obedient son in everything else—but not here."

"Let him go with you if you like, Rayson," said Sir Henry. "His mother and I have spoilt him and now he defies us."

"No, no, father, you will come round to my way of thinking. You know that if I didn't love Rosa to distraction, I am in honour bound to her. You will trust your old friend, Sir William—the highest medical authority in England. I've heard you call him so. You'll trust him when he assures you that Rosamund is as sound in mind as she is lovely in person."

"I would submit that question to a jury of specialists without fear," said the doctor.

Ronald went to Tangley with Sir William. It made him miserable to see the house—in its desolation—emptied of that loved presence which had made it Elysium—but he thought he might have been even more miserable anywhere else. He sat at that hospitable board the image of gloom, too abstracted to reply to the occasional inanities of Mrs. Dalrymple, who was not wise enough to submit to silence as her daughter did, but who insisted upon pursuing the art of polite conversation, about the weather, the political outlook, and the last popular novel.

It was some time after Ronald had left, and the house had assumed its nightly silence, when Sir William, sitting in his library, with an unread book lying open on the table in front of him, was startled by a knock at the door.

"Who is it? Come in," he called out quickly.

It was Rosamund's maid, Wilson, who stood murmuring something near the threshold, and could with difficulty be induced to come into the lamplight near Sir William's table.

"My good girl, I have not heard a syllable you've been saying," he exclaimed impatiently. "Pray speak out! Why are you up so late? Is there anything amiss?"

"Oh, if you please, sir, I waited till the ladies had gone to bed. I wanted to speak to you alone."

"Well, what is it you want to say?"

"It's about Miss Rayson, sir. When I was putting away her frocks yesterday, I found a letter in the frock she wore the day before she left home, and I kept it to give to you, sir, for I thought you were the proper person to have it, although Mrs. Dalrymple did tell me to give her any letters or papers I found about the rooms. I didn't find any, and it wasn't likely I should, for Mrs. Dalrymple had searched every drawer and every nook and corner before she gave me the order."

"Mrs. Dalrymple did perfectly right. And you found a letter in the pocket of your mistress's gown?"

"Yes, sir, this letter," handing him a common-looking blue envelope.

"Thank you, Wilson. Have you read the letter?" with those grave grey eyes fixed on the girl's face.

"Oh, dear, no, sir. I hope I know my duty better than that."

"People do read other people's letters occasionally," said Sir William quietly. "Good night."

Miss Wilson retired with an uncomfortable feeling that Sir William had read every thought in her brain as she stood before him in her neat black silk gown, the picture of everything correct and estimable in her sphere of life.

William Rayson took the letter out of the envelope. It was the anonymous letter, posted at Pentonville, which Rosamund had carried in her pocket all day, and had forgotten at night, after the agitating scene in the park. He read those malignant lines, and the dagger that had pierced Rosamund's heart went through his.

"What devil has done this?" he asked himself. "My Rosa, my sweet girl! I have made it the chief business of my life to shield her from shame and sorrow. I have not let the winds of heaven visit her face too roughly. And hardly have I left her when some nameless wretch drops his poison into her innocent heart, and drives her from her lover and her home."

He tried to think of anyone cruel enough, base enough, mean enough to have committed such an outrage. It was such a motiveless villainy. And he had so carefully kept the secret of his adopted daughter's origin. There was no one living who could have said, of personal knowledge, that Rosamund was not his own child. Across the sad story of her childhood he had drawn an impenetrable veil. The people who had charge of her in her perilous illness, and from whom he took her in his character of her father's friend, had asked no questions. They had not even known his name. They had been handsomely rewarded for their trouble, and had been assured the child would be well provided for, and there was a dignity and power in

William Rayson's aspect when he was in earnest that forbade over-much questioning. Rosamund's identity was lost in the hour that he carried her away from the sea-side lodging-house. Who, then, could know that she was Lady Chilworth's daughter? He brooded long over that question. No one could know. Someone might guess, perhaps—someone who knew the details of the tragedy. Halstead, for instance, who knew of the mother's anguish about her child, might have pieced the bits of the puzzle together; but Halstead had never entertained the faintest suspicion. Who then?

There had been another witness of the tragedy—another of George Chilworth's guests—who had seen him lying dead by the doorway of the gunroom; a man whom William Rayson disliked for his trivial gossip and his effeminate frivolities. But though Honeybill had always seemed to him a poor creature, a fribble, a pushing nobody, whom he reluctantly admitted to a seat at his board, where men of intellectual weight and public consequence were wont to sit, yet he could not think so vilely of Reggie Honeybill as to believe him capable of ruthless cruelty to a girl. Yet who except Halstead and Honeybill was acquainted with the particulars of the murder, and would be likely to fathom the secret of Rosa's birth? Who else?

"It is not because I despise a man for his four-button gloves and his mincing talk that I can believe him capable of such a concoction as this," he told himself. "It is more like a woman's work."

It is more like a woman's work! As the thought shaped itself in his brain there flashed upon his memory the picture of a Sunday afternoon in the gay June weather, and a group that his gravely observant eye had noted on the lawn—his sister, with Reginald Honeybill sitting close beside her, "in her pocket," as Octavia called it, with his smooth, bird-like head and his hawk nose bent almost to her lap as he talked. How eagerly she was listening! They had a secret look, both of them—that look of drawing-room conspirators, which marks the quiet discussion of some racy scandal, a post-mortem on a murdered reputation. He had thought little of the fact, except to wonder that his sister could take so keen an interest in gossip about a world remote from her own life. Reggie's stories were mostly of the top strawberries in the basket.

But now it occurred to him that Honeybill might

have been telling her the story of the Scotch shooting-lodge, might have been remarking upon the likeness between Rosa and the heroine of that tragedy—a likeness which had never struck Sir Henry Halstead's eye, careless of most things apart from the Bar and the Bench. Was that the solution of the problem? Had Honeybill told the story, and was this vile letter Margaret Dalrymple's secret dagger-thrust at a girl she hated?

Domestic treason! Could it be that his sister, his nearest kin, reared by the same hearthstone, had dealt him this foul blow? Could he believe her capable of such perfidy? The possibility would never have entered his mind had he not for a long time questioned the sincerity of her affection for Rosamund. His watchful eye, trained to read the secrets of the mind as well as of the body, had discovered envy and dislike under the assumption of indulgent love. His delicate ear had heard the sour in the voice when the words were sweetest. He had known for a long time that jealousy and self-interest had been too strong to permit the growth of affection. But he had feared no evil act, no concrete unkindness from a sister, however far she might fall below his original estimate of her character.

He had understood and had pardoned the mother's jealousy of her children's rival.

"Had I been childless, her son and daughter would have been my natural heirs," he thought, "and human nature is a poor piece of business. We are as God made us."

Knowing this he had been glad that a time had come for the parting of the two families. He had meant to provide with liberal measure for his sister and niece, to establish her comfortably in the vicinity, where Tangley and its amenities would be well within her reach. He meant this; and if he had not taken the trouble to convey his intentions to her categorically, it was first because he took it for granted she would rely on his affection and his honour for as much as this, and next because his mind had been absorbed by the consideration of his daughter's marriage, and the settlement which was to secure her the bulk of his fortune.

And now there was this stab in the dark to be accounted for, and he tried in vain to shut out the odious suspicion that Margaret Dalrymple's hand had struck the blow. There had been something in his sister's manner since his home-coming that had puzzled him, a certain strangeness, the look that guilt leaves in the face of a feeble sinner. She had done this thing, he thought, and had repented it when done, and was living in fear of the consequences of her act. She attributed Rosa's flight to that cruel letter. She held herself accountable for all that might follow.

"My poor girl!" he thought, "that I should have brought hatred into her home when I wanted to surround her with womanly love."

He locked the letter in a private drawer of his desk, and he determined to free his house from his sister's presence as soon as he could do so without degrading her in the sight of his household; and on the following morning, directly after breakfast he asked Mrs. Dalrymple to go to the library with him for a little quiet talk. Her fluttered assent, as she rose hurriedly to accompany him, with her knitting needles in her hands, those needles whose indefatigable progress solaced the vacuity of her mind—every look, every movement was full of meaning for the trained observer of human weakness.

"Yes, she did this thing, and she is sorry," he thought.

"Sit down, Margaret; over there by the open window

if you like. You look as if you were going to faint. A sultry morning for September, isn't it? I want to talk to you about future arrangements—for you and Octavia. Rosamund's marriage is only postponed. It will come off, I hope, before the year is out, so the sooner we put things upon a comfortable footing the better."

The knitting-needles quivered in Mrs. Dalrymple's hands as she looked up at him.

"You are very kind—William, indeed you have always been very good to me."

"Not so good as I ought to have been, perhaps, to my nearest relation."

"Except Rosamund."

"Rosa stands apart. She is something nearer than kin, she is a piece of my heart. Well, Margaret, I want to be business-like. The time has come, for reasons which we need not discuss, when you and I can no longer live under the same roof——"

"Oh, William!"

The needles dropped from her hands, as she looked at him, pale and with dry lips.

"Oh, William, what have I done to offend you?"

"We will not enter upon that question, Margaret.

We are here to discuss your future, and Octavia's. Wilfred is, I hope, in a fair way to success in his profession, and I shall not forget that he is my nephew. I am an old man; and it is time that I put things on a settled footing."

"But, William, if I have offended you——"

"Peace, Margaret, peace!" he said, with a warning motion of his hand, and a look that silenced her. "I have been to blame for not being more explicit with you at the beginning of Rosa's engagement; but I thought that you could trust me. Well, I am not so rich as the world thinks me, perhaps, for it is prone to exaggerate every man's good or bad luck, but I have been fortunate in my investments as well as in my professional earnings, and I can afford to provide for you and yours without injuring Rosamund."

Mrs. Dalrymple had resumed her needles, but her hands trembled, and tears began to fall upon the black silk sock which she was knitting for Wilfred. She had to lay down the needles, and put her handkerchief to her eyes.

"I shall settle a thousand a year upon you, in trust, with reversion to your son and daughter, and Wilfred will be further remembered in my will, if he continue to deserve my regard."

The tears that had come faster within the last few moments now changed to passionate sobs, and Margaret Dalrymple fell on her knees at her brother's feet.

"Oh, William, how good you are. If I had known! I thought you were unkind—that you meant to turn us out of doors, with a pittance—that we should have to go back to shabby lodgings, to live in the old pinched way—and that Rosamund was to have all——all your wealth as well as all your love."

"We cannot give our love by just measure, Margaret. Pounds, shillings, and pence are easy to deal with. Come, come," raising her to her feet and putting her gently back into her chair. He had seen women at his feet before to-day, women who had prayed to him for the lives of their beloved as if he were God. "Be calm, Margaret, I beg."

"Oh, William, if you knew——"

"I know more than enough. I have the letter—posted at Pentonville the day you went to Lambeth to see your old servant. I know that you have done a wicked thing, Margaret—but you are my mother's daughter, and I cannot think you are a wicked woman."

"And you can forgive me for that wicked, wicked act?" she sobbed. "Oh, what an angel you are!"

"I will try to forgive you, when I have Rosa home again. And now you have to find yourself a house as soon as you possibly can—and when you have settled that question—taking into careful consideration what rent you can afford, which should not exceed a hundred a year—I will see what is to be done about furnishing. And in the meantime, I will transfer the necessary funds to your trustees—who had best be Ronald Halstead, if he will act, and James Reed, my solicitor's son, in whom I have supreme confidence. I leave you to explain everything to Octavia."

"My poor, innocent child! Oh, William, you will never let her know——"

"Anything to her mother's disparagement? Certainly not! But mothers and fathers ought to walk carefully, Margaret. It is a bitter thing to fear the face of a child."

CHAPTER X.

WHOSE heart has not sometimes ached at the sight of poor streets, surveyed thoughtfully from the pleasant idleness of a railway carriage: the endless rows of shabby houses, resembling each other with a hideous monotony, the gardenless, treeless, hopeless streets, straight lines of small dwellings leading no whither? Never a steeple to close the long perspective; an everlasting repetition of sordid buildings, put together as cheaply as the bricklayer's art knows how, covering every square foot of level soil in places that once were marshy solitudes deemed unfit for human habitation. The press of humanity has overcome the unfitness. Humanity can live or wither there, where the frogs croaked and the bittern flew.

In such a street, but one possessing the superiority of present cleanliness, since the houses had been built within the year, Rosamund established herself, so quietly, and with such business-like rapidity of action, that the neighbours hardly knew that No. 7, Tiverton

Street, had been taken, until they became aware of the presence of two women, mother and daughter, both in the plainest attire of the respectable working classes, and to all appearance subsisting upon the earnings of the daughter, who was asserted to spend most of her time at fancy needlework of a superior character, such needlework as Tiverton Street opined was paid for on a high scale "by them Bond Street shops." Their only luxury was a small servant, whom Miss Smith had engaged on the recommendation of the Vicar's wife, a servant who came from the "Home."

"It wouldn't pay to scrub her own floors if she does 'igh class needlework," said the next door neighbour in conversation with the journeyman baker's wife over the way. "She 'as to set store by 'er 'ands."

Mrs. Smith did not attend to domestic duties of any kind, and might be seen sitting by the parlour window on warm autumn days, watching her daughter as she bent over her embroidery frame with a countenance of calm beatitude, almost as of one who had passed beyond the toils and struggles of human life into a dream-world of perpetual peace.

"If she ain't got a tumour she's about the laziest

woman I ever came in contact with," said the baker's wife. "But I daresay it's a tumour. And that would account for the daughter making so much of her."

To make much of mothers was not a usual thing in Tiverton Street, since it seemed in the natural sequence of things that grown-up daughters should trip daily off to the factory or the shop, while mother scrubbed, and washed, and ironed, and cooked, and mended, at home. They, being the bread-winners, the actual wage-earners, took the higher position; and mother's domestic slavery seemed a feeble set-off against her bite and sup, more especially if she hankered after a drop of gin to keep the cold out on damp evenings. The daughters, as a rule, preferred cocoa, and to save their money for a Gainsborough hat.

Tiverton Street, St. Mary's Town, was a curious exchange for Tangley Manor, and for all the graces and adornments of everyday life, choice pictures, delicate china, the mellow richness of artistic draperies and furniture, Persian prayer-rugs, and Japanese embroidery, and the quaint prettiness of old silver. All those luxuries which had surrounded her ever since she could remember, Rosamund gave up willingly for her mother's sake, to see the haggard look gradually leave the beautiful face, the eyes soften with the light of happiness, to hear the tender pathetic cry, "God has given me back my child. *Rosa mia,* I did not know there was such joy in the world."

To have given her mother liberty and gladness, to have saved her reason, perhaps—for it was hard to believe that this calm and equable content did not predict a complete cure—this was Rosamund's mission, and she was steadfast in its accomplishment, not reckoning the cost. She had given up her lover, because it seemed her duty; she had separated herself from her father; and the thought of their distress and the pain of separation from them were hard to bear. But she tried to look forward hopefully to the time when she might be assured of her mother's complete recovery, and need no longer banish herself from home and father. In the meanwhile she took measures to relieve Sir William of anxiety on her account by means of a weekly advertisement in the *Times*.

Every Monday morning there appeared a line in the second column to this effect:—"R. R. to W. R. All well and at peace, in a safe shelter, waiting for happier days."

The wording varied from week to week, but the gist of the message was always the same.

The message was answered by Sir William and by Ronald, with earnest pleading for her return, with the assurance that no one she loved should be injured. To these she replied only with the word, "Patience."

After the appearance of the first advertisement, Ronald went in hot haste to the *Times* advertising office and begged for particulars of the manner in which it had been received. They could tell him nothing on the first occasion, but on the advertisement and his inquiry being several times repeated, they relaxed so far as to inform him that the advertisement was always type-written, and always posted at St. Martin's-le-Grand, and paid for by a postal order from the same office.

Rosamund was lost in the metropolitan wilderness of that inner and outer London, to think of which brings bewilderment, the London of Dalston and Homerton, of Walworth and New Cross, of Mile End and Walthamstow, Barnet and Cheshunt, Hertfordshire London, Essex London, Kent and Surrey London, a labyrinth of thirty miles circumference, a place of seething multitudes and continual change.

Rosamund was lost, and neither Sir William Rayson, nor her adoring lover, nor the most persevering and astute of private detectives was able to find her, though not one of the three abandoned hope or relaxed his efforts. Ronald, indeed, spent his days cycling in unlikely districts, but always seeking pretty and secluded spots, such places of trees and gardens and rural cottages as fancy told him Rosamund would choose for her retreat. The possibility of finding her in such a place as St. Mary's Town never presented itself to his mind.

Alone in the midst of crowds Rosamund and her mother led a calm and monotonous existence, unquestioned by anybody, after the good women who visited suffering and poverty in those endless streets had been assured that these two had no need of their ministrations. They were not in want of bodily succour, and there was a dignified reserve in the daughter's manner which forbade interrogation about spiritual things, or a repetition of visits that were evidently not desired. Mother and daughter went to church on Sunday evenings, and appreciated an excellent choir picked from the working lads of St. Mary's Town, and trained by the Vicar's wife. This much having been ascertained, the ministering Sisters were content to leave No. 7, Tiverton Street, unvisited. They had plenty of bad cases, and sad cases to care for. These two women, both remarkable for their beauty, had no need of help.

The house was sparsely furnished in the simplest style possible for comfort. Everything was new and scrupulously clean, but there was no attempt at decoration. A bowl of autumn flowers on the table was the only grace in a dwelling which Rosamund regarded as a tent that might be shifted at any moment. The furniture was hired from a warehouse in the city.

For the first few weeks of that dual solitude Rosamund watched her mother with keen anxiety, beset by the fear of recurring insanity. Every night when she lay down on her narrow bed, in the room next her mother's, with an open door between them, every morning when she woke from lightest slumber, that fear was present in her mind, and she looked with agonising dread for the coming of the terrible change.

The countenance now so calm and gentle might be transformed in the convulsions of madness; the voice, now low and musical, might ring out in the lunatic's shrill-scream. Imagination pictured the worst forms of mental disease, the violent—the gloomy—the suicidal; but the days went on, and that dread horror did not come. The sword still hung over their heads, perhaps, but the hair that held it had not snapped.

All that love could do to make amends for past suffering had been done by Rosamund; but that suffering had left ineradicable traces. The fear of recapture haunted the fugitive, expressing itself in a vague apprehension, a nervous distrust of a strange footstep at the door, a strange face outside the window. The horrors of the madhouse came back to her in her dreams, and she would lie down happy and at peace, to pass a night of agitation and unrest.

An indifference to everything in life except her daughter's society was the chief note in her character. She had lost all interest in the world from which she had been banished in the flower of her youth. All those years which should have been most vigorous, the fullest of thought and feeling and action, had been spent in a dull routine that reduced the body to a machine and made the mind a blank. She had not been cruelly treated. She had only been allowed to wither in the dull misery of a life without a future, the unending heart-sickness of days that know no change. The consummate passion of her life, her love for her child, had kept her alive, and had devoured her life. The wild hope of escape and reunion with that lost idol had been an intermittent fever of the brain.

And now having realised that hope, finding herself loved and cared for by the object of her love, her contentment of mind seemed like apathy. She had nothing left to wish for. She was completely happy; but the exhaustion of long years of suffering made even happiness seem a dull thing, to those who were ignorant of her story.

She was helpless, too, with an almost infantine helplessness, the keepers having treated her as a creature without sense. She had lost all manual dexterity, and could not dress herself without assistance. Her sewing was that of a child.

"I used to ask them for needlework once," she said, after she had made a vain attempt at assisting in Rosamund's delicate work, "and they gave me some dusters to hem; but the hideous things hurt my fingers, and I hated them. And then my keeper scolded me for being idle. If they had given me anything pretty it might have been different; but now I can't even hold a needle."

The exposure and fatigue of those days and nights during the journey from Scotland, one night spent on an open common twenty miles south of Edinburgh, had left their effect in a cough which was not easy to cure. Rosamund called in the doctor of highest esteem in the neighbourhood. He was an elderly man, who had spent all his working days among the poor, but his face and manner inspired confidence. Rosamund saw him alone after he had questioned and sounded his patient, and his verdict was disquieting. There was weakness in lungs and heart, the possibility of serious trouble, if the utmost care was not taken. Gentle exercises, careful diet, and an open-air life were recommended.

"We go to Victoria Park in the tram every sunny day and stay out of doors as long as the sunshine lasts," Rosamund told him.

"That is very good, but the winter is coming, and we shall have a short allowance of sunshine in this part of the world by-and-by. If you could manage to take your mother to a better climate—Devonshire, for instance."

"Or Italy!" suggested Rosamund. "Would Italy be better?"

"Why, of course it would. Italy, or the Riviera. But I'm afraid you couldn't manage that."

"I'm afraid not."

"No, of course not. Foreign travel is a costly business. Try Exmouth, or Torquay, or Lyme Regis, which is nearer—a pretty sheltered place."

"There is something I want to speak about," Rosamund said, faltering a little. "There was a time in my mother's life when her mind was affected. Do you think there is any fear that evil might return?"

"I cannot answer off-hand, my dear young lady, without knowing the history of the case. Your mother strikes me as apathetic rather than excitable. I'll call again in a day or two, and have a quiet talk with her. You can leave us alone for a little bit."

"I don't think I could do that," said Rosamund, alarmed at the idea of what her mother might reveal in her absence. "I would rather you would talk to her before me. I don't want her to be frightened, or to suspect that she is being questioned seriously."

Dr. Spillman assented, and upon his next visit, three

days later, he stayed a considerable time, engaging Lady Chilworth—*alias* Mrs. Smith—in conversation, and watching every change in her countenance with something of the gravely observant expression that Rosamund knew so well in her father's face. It was this serious aspect of the East End doctor, this tranquil look of thought and sympathy, that had inspired her with confidence in a practitioner unknown to Harley Street and Fame.

"I will write to you, Miss Smith," Dr. Spillman told her on leaving.

She received his letter next morning:

"DEAR MADAM,—My opinion after yesterday's conversation with your mother is that her present state of mind need give you no cause for alarm, nor do I apprehend any recurrence of trouble. Her mental condition, so far as I can judge on so short an acquaintance, has been weakened by past suffering. A certain apathy, and also a certain nervous apprehensiveness, suggest some violent shock in the past which disturbed the mental balance without destroying it. Her conversation is calm and reserved. She suffers from no delusions.

Her eyes and general countenance indicate sanity; but there must have been at some past period a terrible shock to reason, if not its complete overthrow. I can advise nothing better for her than the tranquil existence she appears now to be leading, and were it not for the weakness of her lungs I should not counsel any change; but as the case stands I must urge the necessity of a better climate than London for the coming winter.

"Faithfully yours,

"ROBERT SPILLMAN."

Rosamund had no thought of neglecting this advice. Her difficulty was not the want of money, for she had still nearly two hundred pounds. Her fear was that in moving to any English place her retreat might be discovered. These endless streets, this populous obscurity had served her well, and she thought with terror of the world outside St. Mary's Town.

Her first impulse would have been to take her mother to Italy, hoping that the influence of that lovely land would bring health and joy to the enfeebled life; but here the fear of recognition restrained her. In her annual journeys to and fro between London and Milan she had become a familiar figure on the railway. Station-masters and inspectors, *wagon-lit* attendants and buffet waiters paid their homage to Sir William Rayson and his daughter as if they had been personal friends or servants. On the line by Basle it would be impossible to escape recognition. Other routes might be safer; but there would be the risk of all routes being watched, as her father might suppose that Italy, the country she so dearly loved, would be her chosen place of exile.

A small English watering-place, on the other hand, would offer herself and her mother as a subject for gossip. The madhouse had left its outward as well as its inward mark upon Lady Chilworth. There was a touch of strangeness in her aspect, a something which, over and above her beauty of face and form, set her apart from the herd, and drew curious eyes upon her whenever she appeared. Rosamund had seen the attention she attracted in tramway cars, and in the Park, where people often turned to look at her, and pointed her out to a companion—"So handsome, so strange looking!"

Even the severe simplicity of her dress, studiously

unconspicuous, and appropriate to a humble station, could not disguise the something which made her unlike other women. It was the tragedy of a life expressed in person and bearing.

While Rosamund was considering the question of a winter residence with anxious thought, the kindly old doctor had not been forgetful of her welfare. He was interested in both women, the strangeness and beauty of the elder, the pure and perfect loveliness of the younger, a face unclouded by the knowledge of evil, and to which sorrow was a new thing. He wondered, seeing the traces of suffering on the mother's face, that the daughter's brow should be unmarked by the lines of care.

November had begun with a characteristic fog, and it was time for Dr. Spillman's patient to leave London.

"I wonder if you would like to take your mother to Spain, Miss Smith," he said one morning, in the little talk about the patient that Rosamund always contrived as he left the house. "It is a long way, but I think you might be able to manage it very economically."

"Would Spain do as well as Italy?" Rosamund asked eagerly.

"The place I suggest might do. It saved the life of a very worthy creature—a watchmaker in Clerkenwell, who had all the early symptoms of consumption. He was told to go to the South of France—but the expense made the thing impossible. He tried Devonshire without success, and he was resigned to stay at home and die, when a customer of his—a fruit merchant—happened to hear of his trouble, and offered him a free passage to Valencia on one of his orange-boats. Now Valencia is a romantic old town on the Mediterranean, a gay, bright-looking place, and it is in the garden of Spain. It has occurred to me that if you would like to take your mother to Valencia the passage might be managed, as a favour, on one of the orange-boats—I don't say for nothing, but for a very moderate payment. The voyage would benefit her, and the climate would be likely to suit her, and no doubt you could live much cheaper at Valencia than at Cannes or Nice."

"And the boat would be a cargo-boat," said Rosamund. "We should be the only passengers."

"Most likely. In the case I know the merchant or his son often made the passage on business, and their boats had comfortable accommodation. If you entertain the idea, I'll look up my old patient, the watchmaker, and I have no doubt he would help you to arrange about the voyage with the owners. Of course it is a favour to get a passage on one of their boats."

"That would be very kind of you. Yes, I should like to take my mother to Spain."

"And do you think she would like to go?"

"She will go anywhere with me," said Rosamund, her eyes filling with tears at the thought of that devoted love which asked nothing but the companionship of the beloved. The sacrifice she had made seemed almost a small thing when weighed against this intense affection from the mother found so late, found, perhaps, when the sands of life were running low, and there could be scant hope of peaceful years to make amends for past suffering. Brooding over the story of those sufferings—so vaguely known—Rosamund was more and more perplexed by the mystery of her father's dealings with the sufferer. Her affection for him and her trust in his justice and beneficence were so profound that she could not conceive him capable of conscious unkindness to an afflicted wife. If he allowed her to be detained in a madhouse it must have been because he believed her mad; and yet after nearly three months spent in daily and hourly companionship Rosamund had surprised no sign of a mind distraught. It was extraordinary that the physician's gifted eye could have been deceived year after year. Could it be that escape from that dismal prison-house and reunion with the child she loved had wrought a cure so sudden and complete as to be almost a miracle? That solution of the mystery seemed the most plausible.

Again Rosamund could but wonder at the strictness of her mother's bondage in that house of despair, the comfortless surroundings, the severe gaolers, details which had been casually revealed in the fugitive's rare and shrinking mention of that abhorred place. Her daughter had never questioned her, never encouraged her to talk of the hated years; but those scraps of speech had been enough to give a vivid impression of that past life, and it was a wonder to Rosamund that Sir William Rayson's wife should have been submitted to such a Spartan system. She had so often heard of the comforts of the modern asylum, the indulgences that ameliorate the ills of lunacy, and it was inexplicable to her that all that science and wealth can do to soothe suffering had not been done in her mother's case, or that she should have been placed far away in Scotland, rather than in some pleasantly situated asylum near London.

In three days every arrangement had been made for the Spanish voyage. The doctor's old patient, grateful for past kindness, had obtained the privilege of a passage on one of the fruit-boats, and had settled the question with the captain, who asked only for a ten-pound note to cover the expense of proper provisions for the two ladies, and leave a trifle over for himself, the owner refusing any payment. They were to have the owner's cabin, no member of the firm going on this voyage, and were to be waited on by the captain's wife, who always accompanied him when there was room for her. There would be no other passenger, and Rosa and her mother could make the voyage from London Docks to Valencia without fear of recognition or pursuit.

All that was required was that they should be ready to sail in three days, and about this there was no difficulty, as Rosamund had been careful to procure an outfit for her mother and herself sufficient for any contingency. Everything had been bought at one shop, an old-established draper's in the heart of the city, where she had no fear of meeting anyone who knew her, and where her purchases were not of a character to attract attention. The house and furniture were disposed of in a morning, a quarter's notice given and a half-year's rent paid settled for one, and a payment and order to remove settled for the other. The servant was liberally paid, and parted from her young mistress in tears, hopeless of ever again being so well fed or so kindly treated. She stood on the doorstep looking after the cab that carried the two ladies and their trunks to the docks.

"It's been like a beautiful dream," she said to the next-door neighbour, who had come out of her house to watch the departure. "I used to make them a pudding every day, and they would just eat a tiny bit and leave the rest for me, and we had roast fowl oftener than meat, and never a French egg in the house, or a scrap of salt butter, everything of the best, and never no grumbling—but that particular about scrubbing and dusting! Well, you might eat your dinner off any floor in the house, but as kind and as sweet spoken with it all as an angel from Heaven."

"Do you know where they're going?" asked the next door neighbour.

"No, I don't. Miss was never one to talk."

"But you might have read it off the labels. What's the good of edication to gals like you if yer don't keep your eyes open."

"There wasn't any labels," said Marie, "and education don't mean prying. It means being able to sit and read a nice book of an evening, and to write a nice letter to mother, instead of loafing about the streets with a parcel of hooligans."

For Sir William Rayson, and for Rosamund's devoted lover, that interval of nearly a quarter of a year had been a period of keen anxiety. The weekly advertisement in the second column of the *Times* had been all that made the situation endurable. Week after week the absent girl assured them that all was well with her, and beyond this periodical assurance Sir William had only his confidence in the force of a character which it had been his happy task to form, the balance of a mind which education and association had shaped like his own. He had tested her in small things, and had never found her wanting. Her good sense and conscientiousness, her generosity, her pity and love for all creatures that suffer, were well known to him, and he had no doubt of her power to sacrifice her own happiness in the performance of a duty, and to carry out that sacrifice to the end.

"We must possess our souls in patience," he told Ronald, when the young man's impetuous quest of the beloved, and the highest professional skill, had alike failed in discovering Rosamund's hiding-place. "We must wait. She has unhappily conceived the idea that she ought not to be your wife, and she may persist for a time in her determination to part from you, but I do not think her affection for me will allow her to desert me altogether—nor do I think Lady Chilworth will live long. Her health was broken years ago."

It was shortly after this conversation that the weekly advertisement brought Ronald a new cause for uneasiness:

"Do not expect to hear of me for some time. We are leaving England; but there need be no fear for our safety. We go for reasons of health to a warmer climate.—R."

When that advertisement appeared Rosamund and her mother were crossing the Bay of Biscay, that lion in the path which is sometimes as gentle as a lamb, and which treated the orange-boat as kindly as if it had been the mightiest of modern liners. And from the Bay they steamed through the Pillars of Hercules into a summer sea, and seemed to have left winter and rough weather behind them.

The scent of orange flowers was their welcome to Valencia, where by the kindly help of the ship's captain Rosamund found lodgings in a tall, pink villa commanding sea and shore, which called itself a family hotel—three spacious rooms, with a loggia facing south, and a chamber-maid whose eyes were like a tropical midnight.

CHAPTER XI.

AFTER the appearance of that final advertisement Ronald Halstead had to follow Sir William's advice, and possess his soul in patience, since there was nothing else to be done, but his mode of exercising that virtue was a nomadic existence on the Continent, where he roamed along the shores of the Mediterranean, making exhaustive inquiries at every quiet little health resort which seemed a likely place for Rosamund to have chosen. At all the smaller stations on the Western shore, at all the prettiest spots east of Genoa—at Spezia, at Lerici, southwards to Naples, across to Capri and to Palermo, he searched for his sweetheart; but the idea that she might be in Spain never presented itself to his mind. He knew Rosamund's love of Italy; and he thought that the Italian mother would pine for her native land. To Italian shores, therefore, he restricted his wanderings, and spent the whole of the winter in fruitless quest. Nor had he omitted to avail himself of the only possible means of communication with his beloved exile. In *Galignani,* in the *New York Herald,* in the Paris *Figaro,* in the *Petit Marseillais,* his advertisement had appeared:

"R. to R.—Why are you so cruel as to forsake me? My place is by your side wherever you may choose to be. If you ever loved me, end this miserable separation."

There was no answering line.

"Stony-hearted girl, to use me so!" he cried, and then quick on that flash of anger came the sickening fear: "Is she safe? Does she still live? What dreadful fate may not have befallen her since last she told us all was well?"

He lingered at Naples, restless and unhappy, in delicious April weather, loath to return to England, yet weary of fruitless wandering, when a telegram from Sir William Rayson lifted him from a slough of despond to the heaven of hope:

"Fugitives found. Join me at Valencia, Spain. 'Hotel Royal.'"

They were found. A long letter from Rosamund, written by her mother's sick-bed, had told William Rayson the story of self-sacrifice.

After words of fondest affection, tender entreaties for pardon, Rosamund continued: "Only now that the end is so near, have I felt myself free to reveal my mother's place of refuge. The fear that you would take her back to the asylum was so rooted in her mind that I dared not risk the chance of that fear being realised. It might be that you would not believe, as I believed, in her cure, and that you would think it your duty to place her again under restraint, in that sad captivity which has been her martyrdom. Knowing your noble heart, I knew that only a sense of stern necessity would ever have induced you to let her suffer as she has suffered in those miserable years which of late have seemed to her only a bad dream.

"Often in the happiness of my life with you, my beloved father, I have wondered and dreamt about a mother's love; but never till my poor mother threw herself upon me for comfort and protection did I realise what that love could be. It has been my happiness to make my mother's fading life happy, and it has been my sorrow to watch that life ebb away in spite of all that my care could do to keep her from death. It is not lung-disease nor heart-disease that has cut short her days. It is a life worn out. The end is so near now that we have nothing to fear from fate. Come to us, dear father, and take your last farewell of the wife whom you must have dearly loved in happier days, and who has always spoken of you with perfect trust in your goodness, even while she believed that you would send her back to the asylum. Do not think that she has been neglected in any particular. There is an experienced English doctor here, who has attended her constantly, and who assures me that this place has given her as good a chance of recovery as any other to which I could have taken her. He thinks that she was doomed some time ago, and that nothing that could have been done within the last year could have saved her. She brought me love without measure when she came to me at Tangley, a stranger; and she has won my unmeasured love in return. I thank God that I have been allowed these few months of union with the dream-mother of my childhood. I think your science scorns the theory of thought-transference; but I look back and remember those childish dreams with their haunting shadows, a mother's face, the touch of a motherly hand, the sound of a forgotten song; and I can but wonder whether from her troubled thoughts of me in her distant prison-house, the thought-wave conveyed her image to my sleeping brain. You will say this is nonsense; but you will not laugh at the fancy, and you will come to us, in time to see her in her spiritualised beauty, so frail a shadow of what she must once have been.—Your ever loving daughter,

"ROSAMUND."

This letter brought unspeakable relief to William Rayson's mind. She had not been told the secret of her birth. His girl was still his own. She was still his daughter, looking up to him with filial love. Their relations, so utterly happy in the past, were unchanged. Lady Chilworth had kept the secret of her tragic story. It was evident that Rosamund had been told neither of her paternal parentage nor of her mother's crime.

Those months on the Spanish coast, among orange-groves and olive woods, in a picturesque suburb of the old-world city, had not been altogether unhappy for

Rosamund, in spite of separation from father and lover, and the snapping short of a cloudless girlhood. Such love as the mother brought her child, the hoarded passion of years, the one all-absorbing affection of a woman's heart and mind, could hardly miss its reward. Rosamund gave love for love, and with a deeper tenderness because of the dark shadow that brooded over those days of union, the shadow of the inevitable close. They were together, and her mother was happy, but not for long. All that a daughter's love could do was to cherish and comfort a fading life, to disguise the progress of decay, to ward off physical suffering, and beguile the languid hours with gentle talk and pleasant reading. Never to weep in her mother's presence, never to betray the apprehension of a coming doom! This was the task Rosamund set herself, and her courage sustained her through the long ordeal. Mother and daughter were united heart with heart; but of the mother's past life the daughter knew very little. The invalid indulged in few reminiscences of childhood or youth. Indeed, the only days she ever cared to talk about were those sunlit days at Amalfi before Rosamund's birth and until after her third birthday. Of their removal to England, of the reasons for their residence at Amalfi, she never spoke, and Rosamund, always bearing in mind that mental malady from which she supposed her mother to have suffered, refrained from all inquiries.

They talked of the mountains and the sea, of all the lovely things they saw in their rural drives, of the flowers and the children, the mules jingling their bells in the sunshine, tossing the gay worsted balls that decorated their clumsy collars—they talked of the books which Rosamund read aloud—"Kenilworth," "The Heart of Midlothian," "Ivanhoe," "Marmion," and the rest. Scott's novels and Scott's poetry pleased the invalid, while most other books bored her, and were laid aside after a few pages.

Her mind at forty years of age remained of a primitive simplicity. Its growth had ceased when she entered the gates of the lunatic asylum; and from that hour till she held her daughter in her arms at Tangley Park she had been a creature of one idea—the child who had been banished from her after her marriage. All that George Chilworth had given her, wealth, position, admiring friends, had been as nothing when weighed against that loss; yet she had been grateful to him, and until the crisis of Rosamund's dangerous illness she had submitted to his will.

He was her first and only lover; but although she had yielded to his fiery pursuit and surrendered herself to him, she had never been passionately in love with him. He was her handsome Englishman, her fine gentleman, with ideas and manners that stamped him of a world different from that easy-going gipsy brotherhood in which she had lived since her beauty and cleverness had won her the cheap celebrity of a *café chantant.* She had begun to sicken of those vulgar triumphs before George Chilworth saw her, and she needed no dazzling offer of jewels or luxurious living to lure her from the music-hall stage.

He told her that he was poor, and she was willing to share his poverty, nor did she upbraid him when at the end of the vacation he told her that he must go back to England, and proposed to leave her in Italy till he had improved his professional position and could make a home for her. The interlude of impassioned love was over, and he was his own man again, formal, cold, ambitious, but not without honour and conscience. He swore that he would never forsake her, that however hardly the world used him he would provide for her and her child; and he had provided, to the full extent of his means. But it is doubtful whether he would have married her, on his accession to fortune, had it not been for William Rayson, who had exercised a strong influence over his mind from the days when they were schoolfellows at Rugby. Urged by that faithful friend, reminded of Mariana's loveliness, and of the impression such a wife, trained as he could train her, would make in a society where beauty is the one superlative qualification for success, and loving her as much as he was capable of loving anybody, Sir George Chilworth decided upon an act which he considered of unexampled generosity, and made the *café chantant* singer his wife; but he insisted upon her separation from her child, who was to be cared for by strangers, and was never to know her parentage. Mariana might see her from time to time, but only in the character of a distant relation.

"And I shall never more hear her say, '*Madre mia,*' when she puts her arms round my neck. She was just beginning to speak the words."

"Children soon forget," said Chilworth; "and you

may have another child by-and-by, Mariana, a son, perhaps, who will call you mother."

"He can never be to me what she has been. Think of those years at Amalfi when she was my heaven and earth!"

"Yes, no doubt they were long, dull years, my poor Mariana——"

"Dull! With her?"

"She was your consolation—yes—of course. But your life now is a very full life; and I hope, in justice to me, there may be no repining, or I shall feel that I made an egregious mistake when I legalised our position and brought you to London."

This was a sample of many conversations. It was the only question which ever gave Chilworth trouble in his relations with his wife. In every other detail he found her perfect, quick to learn the usages of society, adaptable, invincible in charm and supreme in beauty, wearing picturesque clothes and splendid jewels with a careless grace which was more telling than the *tirée à quatre épingles* style of most of her rivals. As a wife she had fulfilled all that William Rayson had promised for her. It was only as a mother that she gave trouble.

murmured Rosamund, "and I know how dearly he loved you. I know it by his sorrow."

"He is a good man, Rosa, a good Christian—a true friend. Love him and cherish him, *carissima;* he is worthy of your love."

Sir William was with them at sundown. In the splendour of the afterglow he sat with Mariana's hand clasped in his, and Mariana's child kneeling by her mother's chair, and looking up at him with infinite love.

Few words were spoken between them, the man who had so passionately, so vainly, so faithfully loved this woman, and the woman who had never given him look or word of love, yet who had known that in him she had the one friend of her life. To have had one such friend in a life was perhaps the quintessence of friendship. A legion of commonplace friends would not have been worth as much.

She had always been grateful to him, and she thanked him again this evening, which might be her last evening on earth; thanked him in vague words that betrayed no secret of the cruel past.

"My poor Mariana! I did the best I could," he said, and that was the most he had ever said of more than twenty years of devotion, of something that had gone perilously near to perjury on the lips of a man of sternest truth, of intercession with Home Secretaries and diplomatic handling of meaner authorities, of lavish gifts to underlings and journeys to the asylum; of everything that love could do to lessen the bitterness of doom.

"My poor Mariana, I did the best I could," he murmured.

"And Rosamund—your daughter—will repay you," said the dying lips, and the dying hands put Rosamund's hand into his.

Rosamund and Ronald did not meet until after her mother had been carried to her last rest in a picturesque corner of the strangers' burial ground, where the cypresses pointed skyward from a garden of roses and scarlet lilies that were like flames on a funeral pyre. Rosamund and Sir William were the only mourners who stood beside that foreign grave in the sweet morning air. Ronald had asked to be present, but had been refused.

"There cannot be too quiet a close to that sorrowful life," Sir William told him. "There are only two people in this world who loved her, and it is good that they alone should lay her to rest."

It was while they were walking home from the cemetery that Sir William spoke for the first time of Ronald.

"Your sweetheart arrived at Valencia the day before yesterday, Rosa, and he is longing to see you. I would not speak of him before to-day; but I think you might be kind and see him this afternoon."

"I have no sweetheart, dear father. I told Ronald that all was ended—and I hoped he was content."

"He is not content, and will never be content till my dearest girl is his wife. And you were very foolish to write such a letter, still more so to make up your mind upon such a serious question as hereditary evil without consulting your father, who has some claim to be considered an authority on such questions."

"Father, don't deceive me, don't think of my happiness before Ronald's! My mother was mad —once, mad for a long time, or you who so loved her would not have allowed her to suffer as she did."

There was a silence of some moments, and then with grave deliberation, as of one who is thinking out a problem, Sir William replied:

"Yes, your mother did—at one time—suffer a paroxysm of mania—so sudden—so terrible in its nature, that it was necessary to place her under restraint, and to keep her under restraint for years, lest there should be another such outbreak. But when you came into the world she was young and happy, and in sound mental health. There was no taint of madness in her family, nor had she ever suffered the slightest mental trouble. Perfect in physical beauty and vigorous in mind, she was the fitting mother of a lovely daughter. My Rosamund's husband can have nothing to fear from fate, or I would not give her to him. I have seen too many tragedies of hereditary doom!"

"Father, I have always trusted you," said Rosamund, bursting into tears, in a sudden revulsion of feeling.

"You may trust me, dear, to the end of life."

"Then I should dearly love to see Ronald this afternoon. You know how I have always loved him, but I would have given him up rather than that he should suffer for me as you must have suffered———"

"Hush, dearest! The past is past. Never speak of it again. My dear girl has done her duty to an afflicted mother bravely, conscientiously———"

"I loved her, father, I loved her. There was no question of duty. I gave up my life to her willingly. I regretted nothing but parting from you."

"You will have your reward. Ronald has shown himself a lover in a thousand. And now, dear, as this sad interval in your life is to be a family secret, my plan is that you and Ronald should be married at Madrid almost immediately, and that you should come quickly back to Tangley after a summer honeymoon in the Engadine. All fuss and talk will be avoided—and all the commonplace of a conventional wedding. If people ask later why you were married in Spain instead of in England, it will be for me to answer."

"But my aunt and cousins, father? What will they think?"

"Just whatever they please. They have been disposed of—made comfortable—in a house of your aunt's own choosing—at Barnes. It is a longish way from Tangley, but as I suggested to your aunt, it would be more convenient for Wilfred to run backwards and forwards; and you know that Wilfred is her sun, moon, and stars."

"Yes, poor auntie. She positively worships her children."

Later, Rosamund spoke, falteringly, and with infinite pain, of the anonymous letter.

"There was an anonymous letter, father, which I wanted to show you—only, in the confusion of my last day at Tangley I lost it."

"The thing came into my hands, dear. A crazy letter—of no moment. Let the memory of it never worry you. My girl's life is to be steeped in sunshine, cloudless as this blue sky."

The prophecy was bold, but of all the marriages of that year there was none that began with greater promise than one of which society papers took very little notice, and which the *Times* recorded in simplest fashion:

"On the 1st of June, at the English Embassy, Madrid, Ronald, only son of Sir Henry Halstead, of Hyde Park Gardens, to Rosamund, only daughter of Sir William Rayson, of Tangley Manor, Hampton-on-Thames."

THE END.

CPSIA information can be obtained at www.ICGtesting.com
Printed in the USA
BVOW032244190213

313725BV00003B/251/P